SEVEN GRAVES
ONE WINTER

By CHRISTOFFER PETERSEN

www.christoffer-petersen.com

— Ah, it has hardened
Hundreds of Hearts
Bound for the Pole
of unnameable Pain

Author's translation from
NORDPOLEN
by
LUDVIG MYLIUS-ERICHSEN (1872-1907)

— Aa, der er stivnet
Hundreder Hjærter
paa Vej mod Polen,
af navnløse Smærter

for Isabel

NOTE TO THE READER

Seven Graves, One Winter introduces the main character of Constable David Maratse from the east coast of Greenland. This story, the first in a series, takes place after the events described in book two of The Greenland Trilogy: *In the Shadow of the Mountain*. While some reference is made to that book, it is not necessary to read *In the Shadow of the Mountain* before reading this book. I lay all blame for any confusion firmly at the feet of Constable Maratse, as he was quite insistent, in his own quiet manner, for a story of his own. The characters of Petra Jensen and Gaba Alatak have also appeared in short stories featuring Maratse. It is not necessary to read these stories before reading *Seven Graves, One Winter*.

Once again, it is Maratse's fault.

The people of Greenland speak Greenlandic – including at least four dialects, Danish, and English. In many aspects of daily life, West Greenlandic and Danish are the working languages. *Seven Graves, One Winter* is written in British English with the use of some Greenlandic and Danish words used where appropriate, including:

East Greenlandic / West Greenlandic / English
iiji / aap / yes
eeqqi / naamik / no
qujanaq/qujanaraali / qujanaq / thank you

Sapaat

SUNDAY

Chapter 1

They dug the graves on the mountain's knee, in the stubborn earth pinched between boulders of granite. The graveyard was small, but large enough to accommodate the mothers, fathers, sons and daughters of Inussuk, from the time when the first grave replaced the last cairn, and babies that succumbed to the winter were no longer mummified. The winters were just as dark, the summers just as bright, but the deaths had slowed, and food, from the sea or the store, was easier to come by. But still they dug the graves each long summer, in anticipation of each dark winter when tuberculosis might take a grandparent or a grandchild, when a winter storm might take a hunter, or a depression might force someone to take their own life. They dug two graves for suicide, hoping they were two too many. They dug one for a drunken brawl, one for a fishing accident, one for the stillborn child they knew was waiting in the tiny morgue of the medical centre, one terrible boat ride away. They dug a sixth grave for old age. The seventh they dug for cancer. Even in the Arctic, always cancer.

The men climbed out of the suicide graves and leaned on their shovels for a moment, gazing out at the icebergs in the fjord. The graveyard commanded the best view of the mountains in the distance and the settlement nestled in the lap of the mountain below them. Inussuk was trapped between two beaches, one black and soft, the other shingle, shell and stone. The black beach faced south and east, breaking the waves and absorbing the energy of each storm, littered and glittered as it was with gobs of ice the size of the gravediggers' hands, hearts and heads. The larger ice debris – growlers – studded the beach, and diverted the water running off the mountain and streaming into the sea. It was between two floating growlers that the girl's body would be found a short distance from the beach that autumn, but, at that moment, the gravediggers knew nothing.

They shifted their gaze from the beach to the settlement, picking out the blistered red wood walls of the general store, and the fresh green paint of the house owned by the nature commission, currently occupied by two Danish artists and one small child. One of the men nodded in the direction of the house as the girl played in the sand and dirt beneath the deck. The forty-three adult residents of Inussuk thought the two artists were lovers. The twelve children were too young to care, content with a new playmate, a girl with blonde hair.

"Fifty-eight residents," said the older of the two gravediggers. He reached into the satchel at his feet and pulled out a thermos. A lick of wind off the fjord chased the steam from the mouth of the flask as the man unscrewed the lid. He poured coffee into an enamel cup for the younger man, filling the lid of the flask for himself.

"*Aap*," said the younger man, as he lifted the cup to his lips. He looked down at the settlement, watched the girl playing in the dirt, and then flicked his gaze to his son waving from the dock. The small boy's lips moved and his chest heaved as he shouted and the man waved, reminded as he was every time he saw Qaleraq that the boy was healthy, curious, hellish to teach, but desperate to learn. Qaleraq would see many more winters, unlike his sister's son. They would dig the last grave for his stillborn nephew, the heavy jabs of the spade penetrating as deep as they could dig, to the permafrost if they had the energy for it, so that the boy might rest right down in the earth.

He finished his coffee, flicked the dregs into the grave, and tossed the cup into his partner's satchel. He climbed into the grave and began to dig. The older man poured another half cup into the lid of the thermos, looking around the graveyard as he drank. The antenna mast cast a thin shadow on the graves of his mother and father, the plastic wreaths parched in the polar sun. He made a promise to replace them, the same promise he made the previous summer when they had dug the seven graves, and an eighth in September, just before the first snow of winter. Pneumonia had surprised an elderly couple, the man, Aput, succumbing just a week after his wife, Margrethe. The gravedigger let his gaze wander down the path as he remembered carrying the coffins, one after the other, from the couple's house to the graveyard, before catching his breath during the service and lowering his parents' closest friends into adjacent graves. The path was steep and he knew every turn, boulder and buckle. He had stubbed his toes on rocks, slipped on loose stones, and dug steps alongside the younger man for the better part of six years.

Six years and seven graves each year.

Inussuk was shrinking as the graveyard swelled. The young and educated left the settlement in favour of the larger villages and towns on the west coast of Greenland. The children left for the school in Uummannaq, returning aged fifteen and sixteen after their tenth grade, only to grow bored by the quiet life between the two beaches, and frustrated by the lack of jobs and money. Just one boy had returned to fish the same waters as his father, while his sister and her friend left to study at the Further Education college in Aasiaat, further down the coast.

"Hey," the older man said, as he finished his coffee.

"What?"

"Did you hear about the policeman?"

"Policeman?" The younger man leaned his shovel against the wall of earth and climbed out of the grave.

"He's coming next week."

"Coming here?"

"*Aap*," the older man said and pointed at the dark blue house behind the general store. "He bought Aput's house." He paused. "You didn't know?"

"*Naamik*," said the younger man, and then, "Maybe."

"You should listen to your wife, Edvard. My wife told her."

"Sure."

The older man caught Edvard's eye. "Is something wrong?"

Edvard shrugged. "The baby," he said and glanced to where his son was now playing with the Danish girl. "We want another child, but she is worried that what happened to her sister might happen to her. She says it could be the water."

"The water?"

"Metal, from the mine. It will be in the fish."

"There's no metal in this water."

"You don't know that, Karl."

"No," Karl said and sighed, "I don't." He screwed the lid onto the thermos and pushed it inside the satchel. He gripped his shovel and moved to jump into the grave. Edvard stopped him with a cough. "What?"

"You were telling me about the policeman?"

"*Aap*, he is moving here."

"To work?"

"To live."

Edvard shook his head and said, "You said that already, but will he be working here? As a policeman."

"We have never had a policeman in Inussuk."

"Which is why I want to know."

Karl laughed. "Are you worried about your home brew? If he finds it, maybe there will be more yeast in the store, and I can get fresh bread for a change."

"Maybe," Edvard said and smiled, "but where would you get your booze then, old man?"

"From Uummannaq, like everyone else."

"Suit yourself." Edvard thought for a moment. "But why is he coming here, if not to work?"

"Buuti said he is retiring, something about an early pension."

"He must be ill," Edvard said and glanced at the two graves they had nearly finished.

"Infirm, invalided," Karl said. "I heard he walks with a stick, maybe two."

"So he is moving here from Nuuk?"

"*Naamik*, he is from Ittoqqortoormiit."

"Tunu? East Greenland?"

"*Aap*."

"Why is he coming here?"

"I don't know. You can ask him next week."

Edvard grunted and jumped into the grave. He picked up his shovel and started to dig as Karl did the same in the grave next to him. They worked for another two hours, finishing the graves at the same time, as they always did, although Karl suspected Edvard slowed each time he was almost done, scraping at the edges instead of digging, waiting until the older man was finished.

Karl was the first to climb out of the grave, and he gave Edvard his hand to help the younger man up, a small token of thanks in return for the respect he showed for his elders. They walked to the other end of the graveyard, closer to the edge that reached down the knee of the mountain and to the waves lapping at the dark, wet rock below. They traced the shape of the two graves they would dig here, as close to the edge as they dared, as close as was considered respectful, without condemning the occupants to an eternity of vertigo.

Edvard paused at the furthest corner and looked out to sea. He prodded Karl's shoulder and pointed at a medium-sized motorboat with a flash of lightning stencilled along the hull, bobbing in the shadow of a large iceberg, too close to escape the wave and debris should it begin to roll or calve. Karl sucked at his teeth and Edvard shrugged. Neither man recognised the boat. Even at this distance it would be strange not to know the shape of a local hull, or the curve of its bow.

"Do you know who that is?"

"*Naamik*," said Edvard. "Maybe it's from Disco Island?"

"Maybe."

The two gravediggers rested on their shovels and watched as the boat drifted away from the iceberg and out of view. They waited until the stern disappeared behind the iceberg. Only then did they make the first cut of the new graves. If they could see through or around the iceberg, they would have seen a man struggle into view from the cabin of the boat, dragging a naked girl by her long black hair. They would have seen him slap her twice in the face. If the wind had been blowing in the right direction, they might even have heard her scream.

She was young with soft curves that defined her sex. Her skin was darker than her European friends, lighter than the Greenlanders. She was bruised. Her nose was bloody. The man wiped her blood from his hand on her stomach, before he dragged her across the deck and shoved her onto the floor. She thrashed her legs like a bloody fish, and he hit her again, this time with the back of his hand, slamming the back of her head against the side of the boat. The boat dipped with the impact and her legs went limp as her brown eyes widened and she stared at the man. The girl's hair flowed onto the seat moulded into the hull and the man squirmed the sole of his boot onto the seat, clamping her in place. He reached over the girl and grabbed a bag from the seat opposite, unzipped it, and spilled winter clothes onto her stomach.

"Get dressed," he said. He tossed the bag towards the cabin and leaned on his knee. The girl held her breath, struggling with the overtrousers and socks, as she stared at the man. He removed his foot from her hair and told her to sit up and put on the fleece sweater, and a large, thick, *Canada Goose* winter jacket. As she dressed, his gaze lingered over the dark areolae of her breasts. He dragged her to her feet and across the deck. He reached for a pair of hiking boots beneath the steering column. "Boots," he said, as he threw them to her. He spun the chair in front of the wheel and pushed her hard into it. She bit her lip and he grabbed her by the hair, eliciting a sob as he tugged once and waited for her to pull on the boots and tie the laces. When she was done he pulled her to her feet and marched her to the port side of the boat, the one closest to the iceberg.

The girl gripped the rail along the side, her body shaking as she sobbed. The man released her and returned to the wheel, applying a little thrust to manoeuvre closer to the iceberg. He cranked the engine out of gear and let it idle. A pall of grey smoke drifted across the girl's face and she coughed.

"What's that?" he said.

"I coughed," the girl said in Danish. She could taste tears on her lips, salt like the sea.

"What did you say?" The man gripped her by the hair.

"I said nothing," she said, as he twisted her face to look at him. "Nothing," she sobbed.

"Speak Greenlandic, bitch," he said and jerked her head downwards, smiling as another sob caught in her throat.

"I can't."

"Exactly."

The man pushed her toward the railing. The girl cried out as she slipped to her knees. Strands of her hair caught in the fur ruff of the jacket's hood as the man changed his grip, and jammed his hands under her arms.

"Get off my boat," he said and lifted her up. She screamed, her hands flailing at the railing, desperate for a grip as the man heaved her over the side and her legs slid into the water. He grunted with the sudden weight, his feet sliding along the deck as her fingers caught around the railing and she clung to it. The man kicked at her knuckles until she screamed and let go, palms slipping down the hull of the boat as the air inside the jacket swelled on contact with the water. The cold pressed the air from her lungs and she started to convulse, as she fought for her last breath.

As soon as he heard her splash into the water, the man moved back to the throttle, put the boat in gear, and powered away from the girl. Her eyes bulged as she watched him turn a short distance away, before correcting his course and leaning out over the side of the boat to stare at her. She heard the engine roar as he opened the throttle and sped towards her.

With what little strength she had left, the girl splashed at the water with stiff fingers, as she tried to swim away from the boat. The man corrected course and she caught the stiff hull of the boat on her cheek as the man powered past her. Her head dipped under the water, her hair flat on the surface like tendrils and nerves, plugged into the water, tuning into her death, as the man checked his speed, turned the boat, and accelerated towards her one last time. The keel of the boat clipped her head, the vibration knocking along the hull.

The man smiled, and made a slow circle of the girl's last known position. He settled on the seat behind the wheel and reached into his pocket for a packet of mints, frowning as his fingers caught on the girl's topaz panties. He stuffed them back into his pocket and set a course for the mouth of the fjord, as the gravediggers dug deep into the mountain above Inussuk.

Marlunngorneq

TUESDAY

Chapter 2

Constable David Maratse grunted as another rod of pain shot through his legs and lit his lower back in what he imagined to be a wall of fire. It was the same every time he lifted his left foot, with another flaming rod of pain pressing through his nerves when he placed his sole flat on the treadmill. Maratse paused to catch his breath, white-knuckling the handrails as the physiotherapist made another note on his clipboard.

"It's not getting better, is it?" he asked.

"*Eeqqi*," Maratse said, and shook his head. He took a breath, breathed out, once, twice, three times until the pain subsided. "Again," he said, and lifted his foot.

"You're sure?"

"*Iiji*," he said. "Yes, I'm sure." His nerves flamed and Maratse crumpled, cursing as he fell onto the treadmill's rough rubber surface. The physio turned the machine off and helped Maratse onto his feet.

"Let's get you sat down," he said.

"I've been sitting down for a week."

"And before that you were lying down," the physio said, as he helped Maratse into a chair, "for three weeks. This is progress. You have to take it slow."

"Progress?" Maratse grunted. He patted the pockets of his jogging bottoms, and then realised his cigarettes were in his jacket pocket, beside his hospital bed.

"Smoking won't help."

"It helps me."

"Seriously," the physio said, "with the damage

your nerves have been exposed to…"

"Smoking helps," Maratse said, and dared the physio to suggest otherwise. The young man shrugged and made more notes on his pad. Maratse thought about nerve damage. He could almost smell his own charred flesh, as the Chinese man had pressed the ends of his improvised torture device into Maratse's chest, his legs, his testicles. Maratse shoved the image from his mind and calculated the distance to his bed. "I need a smoke."

"I'll have someone take you back to your ward," the physio said. He put down his pad and walked across the training room to where Maratse's wheelchair was parked alongside the wall. He started to push it across the floor, stopping when the door opened. He smiled at the policewoman as she entered the room, let go of the wheelchair, and said, "He's all yours."

"He's done?" she said, and brushed a loose strand of long black hair behind her ear. The movement reminded Maratse of another woman who did the same, a Danish Konstabel in the Sirius Patrol, the same woman who had rescued him from the Chinese man.

"I need a smoke," Maratse said and nodded at the wheelchair. "One of you needs to help me."

"Still grumpy, eh?" The policewoman said. She sighed and tucked the envelope in her hand inside her jacket, gripped the handles of the wheelchair, and positioned it alongside Maratse's chair. The physio helped her lift Maratse onto his feet, switching the chairs as the woman supported Maratse. She smiled and caught Maratse's eye. "Forgotten my name again?"

"Hello, Piitalaat."

"My name is Petra," she said. "Constable Petra Jensen." Maratse winced as he felt the physio push the seat of the chair against the back of his legs. Petra helped him sit. "Why do you insist on calling me that?"

"I like it," Maratse gripped the circular bars on each side of the wheels. He backed away from Petra and nodded at the door. "I need a smoke, Constable."

"I heard you the first time," she said. "Oh, and it won't be Constable for much longer."

Maratse turned at the door. "Sergeant's exam?"

"Yes," she said. "It went well. I should get the official confirmation by the end of the week."

"Is that what's in the envelope?"

"No." Petra's lips flattened, and she brushed at an imaginary strand of hair. "That's something else."

"For me?"

"I'm afraid so."

Maratse sighed and nodded at the door. "Let's go," he said.

Petra opened the envelope as she walked beside Maratse towards the elevators. "Do you want me to read it?"

"*Iiji*," he said and let the rubber tyres scuff his palms, "but just the highlights."

"All right," Petra said. She traced her finger along the closely-spaced print. "They are going to give you early retirement, on a full pension." She paused as Maratse grunted. "But you won't be a police officer anymore. I'm sorry."

"It's okay," Maratse said. He stopped at the elevators and pressed the call button. He had expected as much, and the morning session of physiotherapy had confirmed what he already knew, he would never be a policeman again.

"Are you still going to Inussuk?"

"*Iji.*"

Petra folded the letter as the elevator doors opened. "I don't understand why. You could go home."

Maratse went into the elevator first, turned, and waited for Petra to enter and push the button for the first floor. "I'll always be the policeman," he said. "It's better to start somewhere new."

"Retired," Petra said.

"Same thing. It won't make a difference."

"So, you're going to give up the bright lights of the city, and leave me all alone in Nuuk?" Petra leaned against the side of the elevator and composed her best pout. Maratse almost laughed, and she seemed content with the wrinkle of skin around his eyes. Petra straightened her back as the elevator slowed to a stop. Maratse waited for her to get out before following her into the corridor.

"What about Gaba?"

"We don't talk about him," she said.

"Since when?"

"Since last Saturday night." Petra walked behind Maratse and gripped the handles of the wheelchair.

"What happened?" he said and let go of the wheels. He caught the smell of alcohol gel as an orderly cleaned his hands outside the men's bathroom, but it was soon gone as Petra picked up speed.

"I don't want to talk about it."

"Okay." Maratse took a breath as Petra spun him around to back into his room. She wheeled him to the bed and Maratse reached for his jacket. Petra walked to the window, leaned against it, folded her arms and glared at Maratse. "What?" he said, pausing as he pulled the packet of cigarettes from his jacket pocket.

"You didn't ask me."

"You said you didn't want to talk about it."

"I don't." Petra turned away and then pointed at the cover of the newspaper on the bedside table. "That doesn't help."

"I haven't read it."

"That idiot from *Seqinnersoq* is mouthing off again. Using Greenlandic as a campaign promise, as a weapon. It's the only qualification he has." Petra picked up the paper.

"When is the election?"

"Next May." She frowned. "You don't watch the news?"

Maratse shrugged. "I don't vote." He pulled a cigarette from the packet and stuffed it into the gap between his teeth. He gripped the lighter in his fist. "I'm going outside."

Petra turned the cover of the paper towards Maratse and stabbed her finger on the photo. "She wasn't much older than her."

"Who?"

"The *girl* Gaba slept with Saturday night." Petra held the paper to one side and stared at the image of Malik Uutaaq, standing beside his wife, with a *gymnasium*-aged girl in the background. "The girl Gaba slept with is about her age, about seventeen or eighteen."

Maratse grunted and wheeled himself to the door. He heard the thwack of the newspaper landing on the bed as he turned into the corridor and continued on to the elevators. Petra followed him. She didn't say a word until they were huddled in the shed for smokers outside the main entrance to Dronning Ingrid's Infirmary. She waited until Maratse had lit his cigarette and then said, "Why don't you vote?"

Maratse took a long drag on his cigarette and then nodded at the front page of the same newspaper a patient was reading while she smoked. He lowered his voice, and said, "I don't trust politicians."

"But you are employed by the government – a government of politicians. We still have self-rule," she said. "You should have a say in who gets to employ you."

"You're forgetting something, Piitalaat," Maratse said. Petra frowned and he continued, "The Greenlandic police force answers directly to Denmark. They," he said and nodded at the newspaper, "don't tell us what to do. Besides, I'm retired." Maratse raised his eyebrows and took another drag on the cigarette. He imagined his nerves relaxing as the smoke filled his lungs. For a moment, at least, he thought he had found peace.

"I hate it when you call me that. It's like you have to remind me I am Greenlandic."

"You are Greenlandic."

"I know."

Maratse puffed a cloud of smoke towards the ceiling of the shed. "I call you that because I like the name."

Maratse finished his cigarette and reached for another. He sighed when he realised he had left his jacket in his room, again. He rested his hands on his thighs and closed his eyes, opening them for a moment when the patient got up to leave. He nodded at her and closed his eyes once more. Petra sat down on the bench beside him.

"What will you do in Inussuk?" she said.

"Fish and hunt." Maratse opened one eye as Petra took his hand.

"But you can't even walk."

"Not yet," he said, and closed his eyes.

Petra squeezed his hand and he curled his fingers into hers, listening to the wind licking at the dust along the street, the caw of the raven scratching on the hospital roof, and the distant peel of a church bell. Maratse felt the wind prickle at the thin hairs on his arms and he was suddenly grateful that the Chinese man had only scarred the skin he did not show, and that the pain was hidden on the inside of his body. He almost laughed at the thought, wondering at the sudden twinge of vanity, curious if it had anything to do with his thirty-nine years and the twenty-something who was holding his hand.

"Maybe I will visit," she said, and squeezed his hand once more, "if I may?"

"*Iiji*," he said, and opened his eyes.

"Will you be all right?"

"I will."

"And you'll stay out of trouble?"

Maratse thought for a moment before answering. From a career point-of-view he had emerged unscathed from his involvement with Konstabel Brongaard and the collateral damage she incurred in her private war with the international intelligence community. It was a wonder he was alive, and he wondered if she was. He admired her guts, her drive, and her moral code, and, for a while at least, he had enjoyed the excitement, the rush of adrenalin so different from his normal policing duties. It had nearly killed him, a fact he was all too aware of, but in the moment – some of the moments – it had fulfilled him somehow. And now, he just had to stay out of trouble.

"I will be good," he said, and let go of her hand.

"Okay," Petra said, and stood up. She tugged a strand of hair from the Velcro at her collar, reached inside her jacket, and gave Maratse his discharge papers. "I'd better go."

"Thanks for coming."

"Anytime."

"Tomorrow?"

"Let me guess, you need a ride to the airport?"

Maratse raised his eyebrows, *yes*.

She nodded and looked at the door. "Can you make your own way back?"

"I can."

"Okay." Petra brushed the tips of her fingers across Maratse's shoulder, turned and walked away. He waited until she had turned the corner before stuffing the envelope under his leg and wheeling himself out of the smoker's shed and along the side of the hospital to the ambulance workshop. He nodded at the mechanic working on one of Nuuk's three ambulances and stopped beside a long, rusted bar, screwed at hip-height into the garage wall. Maratse applied the brakes to the wheelchair, reached for the bar, and pulled himself onto his feet. The mechanic looked up as Maratse cursed the bar to hell and back, before cursing his feet, one after the other, as he inched his way along the wall, and back again.

When the pain was at its worst, just when he thought he might faint, he pictured the Chinese man

21

and his electroshock paddle, and he spat at the wall and cursed the man beyond the white man's hell, and into the frost-burning realm of Greenland's darkest spirits, where seared flesh was a delicacy, and pierced eyes nothing more than an inconvenience before the real torment began.

Maratse paused to pick the flakes of rusted metal from his orange-stained palms, and then gripped the bar again, heaving himself along the wall, spitting at the Chinese man, and cursing the fire in his spine, and the white-hot nails in the soles of his feet.

"I will walk again," he said, and took another step.

He heard the crash of metal as the mechanic downed his tools, and he watched as the man wiped his hands with an oily rag and walked across the workshop to stand behind Maratse's wheelchair.

Maratse gritted his teeth and said, "Just one more."

The mechanic nodded and walked to the row of lockers at the back of the workshop. He returned with a bottle of vodka and two dirty shot glasses, placing them on an upturned barrel as Maratse slumped into his wheelchair. The mechanic poured two glasses and gave one to Maratse.

"*Skål,*" the mechanic said and clinked his glass against Maratse's. He waited until Maratse had downed the first glass, before exchanging his full glass for Maratse's empty one.

"*Qujanaq,*" Maratse said and downed the second glass of vodka. "Thank you."

The mechanic took the empty glasses and placed them by the side of the vodka. He reached for the cap and screwed it back onto the bottle when Maratse shook his head.

"You push yourself too hard," the mechanic said.

"Maybe."

"Yeah, you do." The mechanic cocked his head and stared at Maratse. "Why?"

Maratse pulled the envelope out from beneath his leg and gave it to the mechanic. He wiped the sweat from his brow as the man opened the letter and read it.

"That's why," Maratse said as the man whistled.

"They're going to give you a full pension."

"I don't want it."

"You don't have to work again." The mechanic waited as Maratse took a deep breath. When he exhaled he said, "You want to be a policeman?"

"You want to be a mechanic?" Maratse said and looked around the workshop. He gestured at the man's oily hands, sniffed at the heavy taint of diesel.

The mechanic shrugged and said, "I'm good at it."

"So am I," said Maratse. He nodded at the bottle. "Will you leave that when you go?"

"Sure."

Maratse nodded. He turned away from the mechanic, reached out for the bar, and pulled himself to his feet. The pain lit his spine like a firework and he cursed and spat, until the flame became a rod of lightning, as Maratse raged back and forth along the bar until the sun dipped low in the late autumn sky, and all the vodka was gone.

Chapter 3

Malik Uutaaq pushed one leg out from under the duvet of his son's bed and groaned as he propped himself up on his elbows and blinked at the sunlight streaming through the curtains. He swung his legs over the side of the bed and flinched at the sharp corner of the LEGO brick pressing into his foot. Sipu had forgotten to tidy up his room before leaving for football camp. Malik brushed the brick to one side and stood up, the duvet slipped from his body and he staggered across the room to the door, groaning as he heard the bathroom door shut and the sound of his daughter, Pipaluk, running the shower. He straightened the twist of his boxer shorts, bent down to pick up the t-shirt on the floor, and dressed as he climbed down the stairs on his way to the kitchen. His wife ignored him as he opened the fridge and took out a carton of milk.

"Sleep well?" he asked. She sneered and turned back to her cereal. He opened the milk and drank, pressing his lips into the soft cardboard lip, dribbling milk onto the stubble of his chin. Malik slapped the carton onto the kitchen counter and said, "You have to talk to me sometime, Naala."

His wife dropped her spoon into the bowl and turned slowly to stare at him. She pressed her finger onto the counter and said, "When you stop screwing around, we can talk. How about that?"

"Screwing around?"

"Don't," she said, and held up her hand.

"You think that's why I came home late?" Malik laughed. "Jesus. Jealousy doesn't become you. But if that's what you want to think I was doing…"

Naala folded her arms across her chest and glared at her husband. She started to speak, but Malik stopped her with a laugh.

"Of course, if you lost a few kilos, maybe I would come home more often."

"You bastard."

Naala picked up the bowl of cereal and threw it at her husband's head. Malik dodged to one side as the bowl splintered against the fridge. Milk splattered across his thick black hair, and he flicked a flake of cereal from his shoulder as his wife shoved past him and left the kitchen. Malik smiled, filled the kettle with water and let it boil as he turned on the radio.

He made coffee with a spoonful of instant granules as the presenter started the news. Malik stirred milk into his coffee, pausing at the mention of his political party *Seqinnersoq*, the sunshine party.

"Plenty of that around here," he said, and took a sip of coffee. He listened again as the radio cut to a quote from the party's communications chief Aarni Aviki. Malik smiled at Aarni's nasal twang as he stumbled over a string of points at the top of *Seqinnersoq*'s agenda. The media had already picked up on the communications chief's struggle with the Greenlandic language, exposed the Danish roots of his name, and called him *Arne* at every opportunity. Malik was amazed at the control his friend exercised when they pressed him as they did in every interview. But he knew that there was no better poster-boy for the party than a mixed-blood Greenlander making a significant effort to master the language of the people. Malik took another sip of coffee and smiled at the simplicity of it all. The other parties were forced to comment on healthcare, the economy, and social

25

issues of unemployment and housing, but Malik had managed to keep the narrative on language alone, thanks to the dogged determination of his communications chief.

The water pipes creaked and Malik looked up as he heard his daughter turn off the shower. He switched off the radio, finished his coffee and jogged up the stairs to use the bathroom before his wife. He winked at her as he slipped into the bathroom and locked the door, smiling as he heard her curse before slamming the bedroom door.

Pipaluk was waiting in the car when Malik walked out of the house. He put his briefcase on the backseat and took a step back to admire the American import, a Dodge RAM, the fruits of his labours, and one of the many benefits of not paying VAT on international goods. The morning sun shone on the black bodywork, and Malik smiled at his reflection in the door panel. He waved at Pipaluk in the passenger seat and got in.

"You're so vain, daddy," she said, as he buckled his seatbelt.

"And you're not, princess?" Malik tickled his daughter's ear and flicked the long earring dangling from her lobe. "I thought we said they were for special occasions, only."

"They match my outfit."

"But the teachers don't like them," Malik said and started the car.

"They don't say anything anymore, not since you started your campaign."

"No," Malik said, "I bet they don't."

Malik pulled out of the driveway and turned onto the main road, slowing at the junction. He glanced at

Pipaluk as she checked her social media.

"Remember to bring your winter clothes home today," he said and accelerated up the hill towards Qinngorput.

"I left them on the hook in the cloakroom last year."

"Yes, and your mother wants to check that they still fit."

"She said that to you?" Pipaluk said, and looked at her father. "I didn't think you were talking to each other."

"She said it." He glanced at Pipaluk. "What? You don't believe me?" Pipaluk shook her head and focussed on her smartphone. They drove the rest of the way in silence.

It took barely five minutes to drive his daughter to the new school in Qinngorput, less if he hadn't stopped to chat with one of the young mothers dropping off her son in the kindergarten class. Malik had noticed her before, the soft tone of her skin, the way she wore her make-up, the cut of her clothes. The boy tugging at the woman's hand was a brat, and Malik decided it wasn't worth the hassle, especially as he knew the boy's father. He wished the mother a good day, waved goodbye to Pipaluk, and drove into the centre of town.

"More like a city," he thought to himself, as he waited in a short queue of cars at the roundabout. Fifteen thousand people lived in Nuuk. It had an airport, a hospital, courthouse, an international harbour, and a university. "That makes it a city," he said, as the traffic began to move. "And, boy, do I have plans for my city." Malik glanced at his reflection in the rear-view mirror and smiled.

According to the media and the polls his party had paid for, *Seqinnersoq* had a favourable lead on all the other parties, and was gaining popular appeal, especially in the settlements and villages along the coast. Even on the east coast, one of the poorest parts of the country but regionally linked to Nuuk, the people were responding to Malik's call for a renewed national identity, starting with the language. *Seqinnersoq* wanted Greenlandic as a first language, English second, and the eradication of Danish as a working language.

It was that simple.

But Malik knew that Danish roots were long and stubborn. Thin enough to creep into the seams of bedrock, beneath the ice, like a pervasive wire that could not be pulled out without pulling a huge chunk of Greenlandic history and culture with it. Malik didn't care much for history, and the Greenlandic culture was strong, as was the language, for which he might grudgingly accept that Denmark had played a certain supportive role, especially when one looked at the current status of Inuktitut, the language of the Canadian Inuit.

"But we don't have to mention that," he said, and glanced in the mirror. "Do we?"

Malik's focus was the future independence of Greenland. He felt stifled by the Danish influence on his country. He ignored the hypocrisy of sending his children to Danish institutes of Higher and Further education. It was free, after all. But every time he looked at a world map and saw Denmark written beneath Greenland on the world's largest island, he could taste bile in the back of his throat, and he wanted to be sick.

He took a deep breath and sighed as he parked in front of the Katuaq Cultural Centre, the wave form of the building capturing the curve of the Northern Lights he loved and longed for each autumn and winter. Malik turned off the engine and, though the heart of the American beast was still, his own heart beat to a rhythm that made him sweat and he wiped his brow before getting out of the car. He took another breath of fresh air as he picked up his briefcase from the backseat and locked the door.

Aarni Aviki waved at him from his seat in the café. Malik nodded at him, as he crossed the car park and entered the cultural centre. He paused to order a cappuccino and a breakfast pastry and then made his way to Aarni at the table furthest from the door.

"I heard you on the radio this morning," Malik said, as he sat down.

Aarni folded his newspaper and tucked it into his briefcase at his feet. "Can we speak Danish?" he said, in a whisper. "I have another interview scheduled just before lunch, and I need to just relax for a bit."

"Of course," Malik said. He smiled as the waitress brought his coffee and pastry, waiting for her to walk away before speaking. "I've said it many times, you need to relax more."

"That's rich." Aarni looked away for a moment. "These assholes want my blood," he said, and turned to look at Malik. "Constantly."

"You're an easy target. It makes sense for them to go after you. Besides," he said, "it keeps the heat off me." Malik winked. "Perhaps we should raise your salary, again."

"Sure, that would be nice."

"And," Malik said. He paused to spoon the froth

29

from the rim of his cup. "Perhaps more money would mean more social life? A girl, for example? Something else for the media to talk about. To save them speculating about other things."

"Like me being gay? Is that what you mean?"

Malik shrugged. "Your sexual persuasion is your own business, Arne…"

"Don't call me that." Aarni looked around Malik's shoulder. "If people hear you call me that."

"Relax, *Arne*," Malik said. He took a sip of coffee, licking the froth from his lips as he lowered the cup to the saucer. "I'm just saying you're an interesting guy. But you don't need to be *too* interesting. Greenland is a small country, and a little diversion is healthy in certain situations."

"A diversion?"

"Yes."

Aarni leaned over the table. "You're saying I should be more like you?"

"A little more like me, yes."

"Then you haven't read the paper this morning, have you?" Aarni said and leaned back. He reached for the newspaper and handed it to Malik. "Luckily for you, you're not the only one."

Malik frowned as he took the newspaper. He pushed his chair back to make room to turn the pages, and then studied the front page. "This isn't *Sermitsiaq*."

"No. It's yesterday's *Politiken*, from Denmark. Someone left it on my desk last night."

"Last night?"

"I went back to the office after dinner, to pick up some papers. I found it then. Page seventeen."

The newspaper crackled as Malik turned the

pages. He paused to study the page, his eyes flicking from one article to the next until he found one, circled in blue ink. Malik lowered the newspaper and said, "Did you put a ring around it?"

"No," Aarni said. He turned his cup on the saucer, pushed back his chair, and stood up. "I'm going to have another. Do you want something?" He waited for Malik to answer, noticed the wrinkles on his boss's brow, and decided to leave him to the article. When Aarni came back, the newspaper was folded on the table.

Malik looked out of the window. "Who put a circle around that article?"

"I don't know," Aarni said, and sat down.

"You need to find out."

"Obviously."

Malik turned at the sound of the waitress returning with Aarni's coffee. He crossed one leg over the other and waited for her to leave before saying, "It doesn't mention my name, at least."

"You would have been called for a comment if it did."

"But someone…"

"Wait a second," Aarni said, and held up his hand. If he was enjoying the shift in the balance of power at the breakfast table, he was smart enough not to show it. "Let's talk about diversions, shall we?" Aarni waited as Malik took a long breath. "I have been your shield for a long time now. I think we both know that's why you hired me."

Malik glanced at Aarni, nodded, and looked away.

"But just because the media has their attention laser-focused on me, that doesn't make you immune." Aarni tapped the newspaper with his finger. "The party-culture of Greenlandic politics that *Politiken* has so eloquently encapsulated, is, fortunately for you, largely historical. But parties are not your problem, Malik."

"No?" Malik looked at Aarni.

"Your problem is your exotic taste in women."

"Exotic?"

"Mixed-blood, to be blunt. You like your coffee medium-roasted, not dark. You never drink it black, you want it with cream…"

"I get the point, Aarni," Malik said. He pursed his lips and said, "Spell it out for me, politically."

"Is that necessary?"

"Suppose that it is."

"All right." Aarni nodded. "Let's put it in perspective. The media comes after me because I struggle to speak Greenlandic. They are probing, waiting for me to trip up, and to speak Danish. They will nail me for that, but that's all they have. Being gay would be a minor issue. Sure, I would lose all credibility, and, given the taboos surrounding homosexuality in this country, my political career would be ruined. But not my career. This campaign has put me in the spotlight…"

"I put you in the spotlight," Malik said and stabbed the table with his knuckle.

"You did, and I am grateful, and I will show you just how grateful I am, and…" He paused as a text message vibrated into his smartphone. Aarni read the message, nodded once, and finished his sentence, "loyal," Aarni said and smiled as Malik looked at him. He closed the message screen on his phone and slipped it into his pocket. "But the political fallout for you will be far greater. You have made it no secret that Greenland is for Greenlanders, and that means speaking the language."

"The people expect that."

"Sure, and you get a charge from that, a buzz. It makes you feel powerful."

Malik snorted. "You forgot *omnipotent*."

"However it makes you feel, it is also your Achilles heel. Your weakness. Your lust makes you weak…"

"Weak?"

"Yes, because your taste in young Greenlandic women of mixed blood makes you the biggest political hypocrite Greenland politics has ever seen," Aarni said, waving off Malik's response. It was his turn to rap his knuckle on the table. "Greenlanders might denounce and raise a ruckus about political misappropriation of funds, nepotism, and under-the-table deals, but they will forgive and forget when they take everything into consideration – when they are reminded about just how many things a politician has to be good at today, how many skills they need to master, how complicated and complex our society has become. But you…" Aarni paused to lean back in his chair, "when it comes to you they will say *he had one job*. Just one job. Greenland for Greenlanders, speaking the language of their country. If you screw just one more Danish-speaking girl, they will find out, and that will be the end of your career – political or otherwise."

Malik pushed the handle of his cup with his finger, turning the cup on the saucer until the handle pointed at Aarni. He looked his communications chief in the eye and said, "You said you were grateful, and loyal."

"I did. I am," he said. "I have been."

"Have been? Have been loyal, you mean?"

"I mean that when the time comes, you will be able to see the depths of my loyalty. Without a doubt. It's the least I can do. My career is set," Aarni said, and smiled. "For that, I am grateful."

"Then I need you to do something."

"Anything."

Malik nodded at the newspaper. "Find whoever put a ring around that article. Find out what they know, and what they want. Do that for me."

Chapter 4

Nivi Winther's office was on the second floor of the government building beside the police station in Nuuk. As Greenland's First Minister and party leader for the Greenlandic social democrats, she was accustomed to a busier schedule than the members of Greenland's minority parties, but she often longed for the slower pace of the small settlement where she was born. Even Ilulissat, the largest town in the north of Greenland, was more relaxed than the capital, and she looked forward to her visit scheduled for the weekend. Nivi leaned forwards at her desk and tapped the photo of her daughter, Tinka, arms wrapped around her father, Nivi's ex-husband, Martin. People said Nivi and Tinka looked like sisters. She smiled at the thought, and then glanced at the image of Martin, the tall Dane from West Jutland.

"That's who you get your long legs from, Tinka," she whispered, just a moment before her assistant knocked on the door and walked into her office.

Daniel Tukku walked across the pine floor to Nivi's desk, arranged three thin folders in front of her, and tapped each one in turn. "Unemployment. Housing. Culture and identity," he said. "You have ten minutes before the interview."

"And he is only going to ask me about these three topics?" Nivi said and reached for the first folder. She flicked it open with a long nail, smooth with a clear varnish.

"That's what we agreed." Daniel tapped the third folder. "But this is the one."

"Culture and identity?"

"And language."

Nivi looked away and sighed. "Story of my week."

"And every week from now until the election. You had better get used to it."

"They can't move on, can they?"

"Malik Uutaaq doesn't want to move on." Daniel shrugged. "He's got you where he wants you, and the whole country is watching."

"But they don't all agree with him."

"Outside Nuuk? Maybe they do."

Nivi pushed her chair back and stood up. She padded to the window in bare feet, looked out at the sea, squinting at the hazy horizon. "How do we change the narrative?"

"Honestly, I don't think you can. It's personal. He wants it to be personal. And if I was him…"

"You would do the same. I know," she said and turned around. "Remind me again why you chose to work for me."

"Because you can make a difference. Because you won't let language interfere with identity."

"I speak Greenlandic."

"And so do I, but Danish is convenient." The corner of Daniel's mouth twitched. "Should we switch to Greenlandic?"

"Will that make me more appealing to the voters?"

"Malik's voters? No. They listen to him. And each time you beat him in the polls…"

"He reminds the nation that I married a Dane, and have a daughter who only speaks Danish." Nivi shook her head. "It's not fair, Daniel."

"You're right. It's not. Which is why," he said and gestured at the folders on her desk, "I arranged the interview."

"That I have to give in Danish."

"Because the journalist is deaf, Nivi. That's why."

"You couldn't have found another?"

"Qitu couldn't be more Greenlandic. The people listen to him. He has the sympathy vote. Something I will exploit quite happily if it helps us."

"But he does speak Greenlandic?"

"Yes, but it's easier for him to lip read in Danish. Greenlandic dialects can be a problem."

"Remind me again how he lost his hearing?"

"Jumping between the ice floes in the harbour as a child. He fell in the water." Daniel smiled at the memory of a similar experience. "What could be more Greenlandic than that?"

"Sure, you're right." Nivi sat down at her desk. "How long do I have?"

Daniel looked at his watch, and said, "Five minutes. Ten if I offer him coffee."

"Do that," Nivi said, as she opened each folder in front of her. She started to read as Daniel left the office. He closed her door with a soft click.

Nivi skimmed the memo on housing, nodding at each of the bullet points. There was nothing new. Unemployment was another matter, and the promise of jobs in mining and oil was a constant source of optimism in the media, second only to the debate on identity. But Nivi found it difficult to be optimistic when Greenland was dependent on foreign skills and technology. She wanted to boost tourism, but there were only so many jobs the tourist industry could support.

"These are the issues we should be debating," she said, surprising herself at the sound of her own voice.

She looked up, half expecting Daniel to nod and agree with her. But she was alone, and the last folder tugged at her conscience. She looked at it, and then picked up her smartphone from the desk. She thumbed through her messages, and then checked her daughter's Facebook page. There were no new updates. Nivi resisted the urge to call Tinka, just to check in. She put her phone down and picked up the last folder, skimmed the notes and stood up. Daniel knocked on her door a second later.

"Ready?" he said, as he leaned around the door.

"Sure." Nivi pulled on her boots and zipped them to her calves, slipped her smartphone into the back pocket of her jeans, and collected the folders into a pile. She gave them to Daniel on her way out of her office. "Where is he?" she asked.

"Conference room."

"What's his last name?" she said as they walked.

"Kalia."

"Okay." Nivi paused at the door to the conference room, teased her fringe with long fingers, and took a breath. She smiled at Daniel, and then opened the door.

"Qitu," she said, as she strode into the room and shook the journalist's hand. "I'm so pleased you could come. She waved at Daniel to close the door and then sat down.

Qitu brushed pastry crumbs from his shirt and sat opposite Nivi. He pushed his coffee and plate to one side and opened his notepad. Nivi caught herself looking for the tape recorder journalists usually had with them. She stopped, leaned back in her seat, and waited. Qitu's voice, when he spoke, was deeper than she had expected. Nivi looked at his mouth, noticed the clean cut of his jaw, and then she saw his eyes, and for the second time found that the journalist had surprised her. She was off-guard, and Qitu's opening question put her on the defensive.

"Tell me about your daughter," he said, his pen poised above the notepad, his dark brown eyes focussed on her mouth.

"My daughter?"

"Yes. Tell me about her."

"You don't want to talk about housing? Unemployment?"

He shook his head. "This is a personal piece. Your assistant said Greenland needs to get to know you. That's why I am here."

Nivi turned to look at the door, but Daniel had closed it. She looked at Qitu, thought for a moment, and said, "All right. What do you want to know?" She paused as Qitu took a sip of coffee.

"Tell me about your daughter."

"Tinka?" Nivi smiled. "She's seventeen. She's in her second year of *gymnasium*, high school."

Nivi watched as Qitu made notes with barely a glance at the notepad. She felt, for the first time in her life, that she truly had someone's attention, as Qitu focussed on her, on what she was saying. Nivi began to relax. She poured herself a cup of coffee, warming her hands around the base of the cup. She took a sip and then started to speak.

"I said she was seventeen, but Tinka acts like she is in her twenties." Nivi smiled at the memory of the thousands of disagreements they had had on a Friday night in Ilulissat, before Tinka had moved to Aasiaat to study, and Nivi had moved to Nuuk. "I have to remember that she is a young woman, and not my little girl."

"When did you last see her?"

"When?" Nivi frowned and leaned forwards. "In the summer, before school started. We spent two weeks in Greece, and then a weekend in Nuuk."

Qitu made another note. "When did you last speak to her?"

"Hey," Nivi said, and put her cup on the table, "what is this about?"

"I am just asking about your daughter. When you last spoke to her."

"Thursday night. Why?"

"Before the weekend?"

"Yes. That's where Thursdays are, every week." Nivi turned as Daniel opened the door.

"Everything all right?" he asked.

"What's going on, Daniel?"

"What do you mean?"

"He wants to know when I last spoke with Tinka." The rubber feet on the legs of her chair burred across the pine floor as Nivi stood up. She pulled her smartphone from her pocket and dialled her daughter's number, glaring at Qitu as she waited for Tinka to answer. Nivi started to tap her foot, pressing redial when Tinka didn't answer the first time.

"She's probably in class," Daniel said when Nivi lowered her phone.

Nivi stared at Qitu. His eyes had lost their initial appeal, and she found herself far less impressed by his note-taking skills, and far more concerned with his motives. Daniel approached the table. She ignored him, folded her arms across her chest.

"Tell me why you want to know," she said.

Qitu stared at her, and then glanced at Daniel.

Nivi tucked her hands around her ribs. She could feel the edges of the smartphone pressing into her skin. She glared at Qitu. "Tell me."

"I'm working on a story."

"About Tinka?" Nivi took a step towards the table.

"Nivi," Daniel said, his voice soft, but urgent.

"Close the door," she said. She waited until she heard the door click closed. "Tell me about the story."

Qitu reached into the satchel at his feet and pulled out a copy of the Danish newspaper, *Politiken*. He laid it on the table, opened it, and tapped an article with his finger. Nivi leaned over the table and started to read. Daniel waited until she was finished and then turned the newspaper so that he could read the article.

"Parties?" said Nivi. "You're writing a story about parties with politicians in Greenland?"

"Yes," Qitu said.

"And," Daniel said, with a glance at Nivi, "you think Tinka has been to one of these parties?"

"Not just one."

Nivi turned away from the table and dialled Tinka's number again. She gave up on the third try and called another number, turning to stare at Daniel as she waited. "*You* arranged this interview," she said.

"I know."

"So she goes to parties. She's a young woman." Nivi tapped her foot. "What's your point?"

"I know. I'm sorry. Shall I ask Qitu to leave?"

Nivi raised her hand and started to speak into the phone. "Martin? Hi. Listen, I need to speak to

Tinka." She waited for a moment, nodded, and then said, "Okay, get back to me with Kaka's number, will you? Thanks." Nivi ended the call and looked at Qitu. "She's been with a friend all weekend."

Qitu nodded, folded the newspaper, and closed his notepad. He stood up, slung his satchel over his shoulder, and slipped his notepad inside it. "You can keep the paper," he said, and walked towards the door. He reached for the handle and stopped to turn around. "I'm sorry."

"For what? Accusing my daughter of partying with politicians? That's hardly a crime."

"You're right. It's not."

"Then why are you so interested?" Nivi frowned and tugged at her lip. She lowered her hand and pointed at Qitu. "There's more to this, isn't there?" She took a step forwards. "What are you not telling me?"

Qitu glanced at Daniel, and waited for him to nod. He looked at Nivi. "I'm doing a story about Malik Uutaaq."

"And?" she said. "Don't look at Daniel. Tell me what this has to do with my daughter."

"Uutaaq was in Ilulissat last weekend," Daniel said.

"That's not unusual," Nivi said. "He has a schedule like the rest of us. He was at a meeting. At Hotel Arctic. You told me, Daniel. You were at the same meeting."

"I did. He was. But he stayed over the weekend."

"And went to a party with my daughter?"

"Maybe, I don't know. But if he..."

"If he *what?*" Nivi said, her voice quavering as her heart started to pound in her chest.

Daniel swallowed and looked at Nivi. "If he was there," he said, "and if your daughter was there too, then," he paused for a breath, "we could use this."

"Use this? Use what?" She looked at Qitu. "Are you writing a story about Malik Uutaaq and my daughter?"

Qitu nodded. "Yes," he said.

"Why? Because you think..." Nivi stopped as she realised what it was that the two men were thinking. She felt the colour drain from her face and then swiped at the screen on her smartphone.

"Nivi, wait," Daniel said, and took a step towards her. She raised her hand, her finger extended, a warning. He stopped. Nivi placed her phone to her ear and waited, lowering it again when Tinka didn't answer.

"Okay," she said, and took a long breath. "Okay. You want to tell me something difficult, so tell me."

"Tell you what?" Daniel said.

"You know what."

Qitu walked to the table and sat down, twisting his satchel into his lap like a shield. "We think your daughter had sex with Malik Uutaaq." He waited for Nivi to respond. She pursed her lips and nodded for him to continue. "More than once," he said.

"And you want to use this," she said and looked at Daniel, "because he had sex with my daughter?"

"No," Daniel said and shook his head. "I'm sorry it was your daughter, but that's not why we want to use this."

"Then why? I don't understand."

Daniel sat down at the table and beckoned for Nivi to do the same. She placed her phone on the surface, stared at it, and then turned it face down to hide the screen.

"Nivi," Daniel said.

"Yes?"

"Malik has the popular vote. He has taken the perceived moral high ground."

"In his position on language and identity? It's pathetic."

"And anti-Danish, anti-colonial."

"We are not a colony," Nivi said.

"That depends on how you view our relationship with Denmark," Qitu said.

"Denmark is a long way from the settlements," Daniel said.

"So is Nuuk," Nivi said.

"True, but Nuuk is still Greenland."

"And you think that the election will come down to that? A choice between pro-Danish parties and the popular nationalist vote?"

"Think about it, Nivi," Daniel said. "You know it will."

"Malik's policy is based purely on the language he speaks. He's in it for the power. He doesn't have an ounce of leadership skills, or the experience to balance a simple budget."

"None of that will matter, if the people think he wants only what is best for Greenland."

"You mean independence."

"Yes. I do. And we're not ready. You know that. There's no oil, and the Chinese want our mines for themselves. There are no jobs." Daniel paused. "We have to stop him, Nivi. We have to discredit him."

"With my daughter, Daniel. You are going to use her?" She snorted. "Have you thought, even for a second, how that reflects on me? It makes him look strong. If he can sleep with his opponent's daughter, he can do anything."

"I don't think he knows who she is," Qitu said.

"What?"

"He didn't sleep with her because she was your daughter. He slept with her because he finds her attractive."

"Lots of girls are attractive."

"But Malik Uutaaq only sleeps with a certain kind." Qitu waited for Nivi to ask what kind, but it wasn't necessary. He realised, as he caught the flicker of recognition in her eyes, and the twitch of a muscle in her cheek.

Nivi thought of her daughter's long legs, her pale cream skin, her long, soft black hair, and her thin European eyebrows. She nodded, and said, "He likes Danish girls."

"No," Daniel said, "he likes half and half, the very people he says are not Greenlandic, because they either have mixed parents, or…"

"They speak Danish." Nivi looked at Daniel and Qitu. "I understand," she said. Nivi stood up, picked up her phone and walked to the door.

"Nivi?" Daniel said. He gestured at Qitu. "The article?"

She shook her head, and left the room.

Pingasunngorneq

WEDNESDAY

Chapter 5

The garage doors of the workshop squealed as the mechanic opened them. He beckoned to Petra, stepped to one side for her to pass, and pointed at the railing on the wall in the corner of the workshop.

"That's where I left him," he said. He pointed at the empty bottle of vodka discarded on the floor. "Looks like he finished it."

"Looks like it," Petra said. She peered into the gloom and looked around for a light switch. The mechanic turned on the lights and she nodded her thanks. She found Maratse's empty wheelchair, and walked to the front of the ambulances to find Maratse lying face down on a pile of jackets and boots. Petra knelt beside him. "Hey," she said. "Time to wake up." She curled her fingers around his shoulder. Maratse grunted and tried to roll away, but Petra held on. "Come on. You've got a plane to catch."

Petra examined Maratse as she might a drunk on the street. She took his hands, turning them gently towards the light, before picking at the bloody flakes of rust in his palms. Maratse opened his eyes and watched her.

"You could have used the gym in the hospital," she said, with a glance at the bar on the wall.

"I like it here," he said.

"You like sleeping here too?"

"It's quieter than the ward."

Maratse started to sit up and Petra helped him. He pressed his hand to his head and shut his eyes for a moment. Petra smiled when he opened them.

"Breakfast will help your head."

"You think so?"

47

"Yeah, I do. My treat," she said, and stood up to get Maratse's wheelchair. He glared at it as she pushed it towards him.

"I need my sticks."

"Which are in your room, on the ward." Petra helped Maratse into the chair. "The sister thought you had discharged yourself, until she found your jacket. She figured you wouldn't have left without your cigarettes."

"Hmm," Maratse said. He flexed his hands around the wheels, and then placed them in his lap. "You drive."

Maratse nodded at the mechanic as Petra wheeled him out of the workshop and onto the road. She turned into a shaft of sunlight stretching between the buildings and Maratse squinted in the glare. Petra turned again, and then pushed him inside the hospital all the way to the elevator. She let go of the chair, pressed the button for the first floor and leaned against the side. Maratse glanced at her and then looked away.

"Your hands are a mess," she said. "Do you want someone to look at them?"

"*Eeqqi.*"

"What about your legs? Are you in pain?"

"No more than usual."

"When did you last take your tablets?"

Maratse shrugged. "Before the vodka."

"I didn't think you drank."

"I wasn't drinking."

"No?"

"I was medicating."

"That's what the tablets are for," Petra said, as the elevator doors opened. She pushed him into the corridor, onto the ward and into his room. "I can wait while you shower." She leaned against the windowsill and the sun caught the loose strands of her hair escaping the ponytail pinched tight at the back of her head.

"Why are you here, Petra?"

"To take you to the airport. Like we agreed."

"That's this afternoon."

"I know."

"Then why are you here?"

Petra stuffed her hands inside the deep pockets of her police jacket. She fidgeted for a moment, as if unwilling to speak. "The Commissioner asked me to look out for you. He knows we've worked together in the past. I told him we were friends, and that I would like to help you."

"Hmm."

"You were tortured, David. It's okay to have a little help."

Maratse lowered his head and studied his palms. He picked at the flakes of rust in the blood lining the creases in his skin. "He asked you?"

"Yes." Petra paused. "After I suggested it."

"You suggested I needed looking after?" Maratse said and looked at Petra.

"Don't you?"

Maratse shrugged, and said, "Maybe."

"Then let me help you. At least until your flight."

"Okay, but no shower."

"I'm not helping you in the shower." She laughed.

"I didn't ask you to. I just don't want a shower."

"You stink, David."

Maratse grunted and wheeled himself to the chair

by his bed. He pressed the brakes into position on the chair and reached for the sticks leaning against the wall. He heard Petra move to help him. She stopped when he shook his head. "I have to do it on my own," he said, and struggled to stand up. After wobbling for a moment, Maratse found his balance, pulled on his police jacket and took a cigarette from the packet in his pocket. He rolled it into the gap between his teeth and grinned at Petra. "Ready?" he said.

"Just waiting for you, old man."

"*Iiji*," he said and grabbed his walking sticks. He pinched the cigarette between his teeth and hobbled towards the door. Petra followed, moving to walk by his side as they walked down the corridor and into the elevator.

"What about checking out?" she said. "Do you want to do that later?"

"I just did," he said, as the elevator doors opened. He walked inside and leaned against the rear wall. Petra shook her head and followed him inside.

"Are you always this difficult, or is it because you woke up beside an ambulance?"

"Always," he said, as the doors closed.

Maratse found a rhythm as they walked to Petra's police Toyota. She opened the door to the passenger side and he grunted as he climbed up and onto the seat, stuffing his sticks beside his right leg as Petra shut the door.

"I'm amazed," she said, as she climbed in behind the steering wheel. "You haven't lit that yet."

"Can't," he said.

"Why not?"

"Too much vodka."

Petra laughed as she started the engine. "You're impossible."

Petra drove through town and parked outside a café by the water. Small boulders of ice stranded on the rocks at low tide shone in the sun, as Petra helped Maratse out of the car and into the café. They sat at a table in the window and ordered breakfast.

Maratse stuffed his cigarette into his pocket and drank black coffee as they waited for their order. He was quiet, content to listen to Petra talk about the Sergeant's exam, as he watched the gulls and ravens fighting over the remains of a seal carcass on the rocks. He looked up when their food arrived and Petra stared at him.

"What?" he said.

"I asked you where you are going to live in Inussuk?"

"I'm renting a house. The grandparents of one of the nurses' died last winter. The house is empty."

"Just like that?"

"*Iiji.*" Maratse frowned. "What is the problem?"

"You have no things."

"The house is furnished."

"But your clothes, other stuff."

Maratse shrugged. "What do I need?"

"Won't you miss anything?"

"Maybe," he said, and finished his coffee. He refilled the mug from the cafetière on the table.

"Like what?"

"A book."

"Just one?"

"Books. I like science fiction."

"Really?" Petra laughed. "You should read crime. All police officers read crime novels."

"I'm not a policeman anymore." Maratse looked out of the window, sipped his coffee, and said nothing more until Petra said it was time to leave. She paid for breakfast and followed Maratse out of the café. He walked past the police car towards the water, stepping over the salty beam of wood separating the wooden jetty from the concrete and asphalt parking area. Petra followed him to the end of the jetty, standing quietly beside him as he looked out to sea.

"If things were different," she said.

"They are not."

"No, but if they were, would you stay in Nuuk?"

"And do what?" Maratse turned his head towards the sun and closed his eyes.

"I don't know. Work in the library, maybe, or in the bookshop."

Maratse opened his eyes and looked at Petra. He nodded at the icebergs further out to sea, and the fine mist of a humpback whale blowing air out of its lungs at the surface. "I can't work in the city," he said. "I need to be out there."

"At sea?"

"At sea. On the ice."

"But the sea is here, too. We just a saw a whale."

Maratse pulled the cigarette from his pocket, tucked it between his lips and lit it. He rolled the filter into the gap and flicked at it with his tongue. Petra moved to one side to escape the cloud of smoke he puffed from his lungs. Maratse grinned and pointed towards the land and the buildings rising up from the street.

"I don't want to live here," he said.

Petra opened her mouth to speak, only to stop as her phone began to ring. She answered the call, nodded, and then slipped the phone back into her pocket.

"They need me at the station. A missing person's case," she said. "I won't be long. Do you want to wait here?"

"I can wait," he said and nodded. He watched Petra jog back to the police car, then turned back to hunt for the whale between the icebergs.

The whale dived deep, blowing circles of air in front of it as it swam for the surface, mouth open, closing its massive jaws on a bounty of tiny shrimps, krill from the bottom of the iceberg. Maratse watched the whale feed three more times before flicking the butt of his cigarette into the sea and grabbing his sticks. He hobbled back to the car park and then struggled along the shore in the direction of the statue of *Sassuma Arnaanut*, Sedna, the mother of the sea. Petra found him an hour later on a bench beside a rack of skin-on-frame kayaks, the Greenlandic *qajaq*, as the tide turned and lapped at the base of the ice boulders surrounding Sedna. She had a package in her hand and gave it to Maratse.

"What's this?" he said and unwrapped the paper.

"A book." Petra bit her lip and wrinkled her brow. "In English. I'm sorry. They didn't have anything else." She sat down on the bench beside him. "Can you read it?"

"I'm a little rusty."

"I'm sorry," she said, and reached for the book. "I can take it back."

"*Eeqqi.*" He smiled. "I have time." He fanned the pages and laughed. "A lot of time, luckily. *Qujanaq.*"

"You're welcome."

"What about the missing person?"

"You want to know?"

Maratse shrugged. "*Iiji.*"

"It's interesting, actually. You know Nivi Winther? The politician? It's her daughter. She hasn't heard from her in a few days, and neither has the father." Petra stood up. "I have to work on this now, so…"

"You need to take me to the airport?"

"Yes. I'm sorry."

Maratse handed her the book as he grabbed his sticks and stood up.

"Do you have everything you need?"

He checked his pockets. "Wallet, cigarettes…" Maratse paused to nod at the book. "Something to read. *Iiji,*" he said, "I have everything."

"Okay," Petra said. She walked beside Maratse to the car, opened the door and waited for him to get in. Neither spoke on the way to the airport, and, as Petra slowed to a stop outside the door to the airport building, her phone vibrated. She ignored it, searching for something to say to Maratse, until the phone stopped vibrating and he opened the passenger door. "Wait, I'll help you," she said, and opened the driver door. She jogged around the front of the Toyota as Maratse found his balance on his sticks.

"I'm okay," he said.

"I know. But I want to help."

"You don't need to."

"I want to," Petra said, and she tilted her head to catch Maratse's eye. "If you stayed…"

"I would get bored."

"With me?" Petra whispered, and for a moment she thought Maratse had not heard her. He leaned against the car, let go of one of his sticks and took

Petra's hand.

"*Eeqqi*, not you. Nuuk." He squeezed her hand. "Thank you, Piitalaat."

"I'm getting used to you calling me that," she said, and let go of his hand to hug him. "The only one I'll allow." Petra's hair caught in the light stubble on Maratse's cheeks. When she let go and took a step back, her hair lingered, until a light wind flicked her hair from his face and severed the connection. Maratse grinned and stuck a cigarette between his teeth.

"Goodbye," he said. He reached inside the police car and tucked the book under his arm.

"I hope you enjoy it," Petra said, with a glance at the book. Her phone began to vibrate, and she pulled it out of her pocket with one hand, waving with the other. Maratse closed the passenger door and waited for her to drive away. He walked to the side of the building and joined the other passengers having a last smoke before their flight.

Maratse leaned against the wall and looked at the book in his hands. It was heavy. The pages spanned the width of his four fingers. He whistled at the page numbers, over a thousand, and then laughed at the name: *The Neutronium Alchemist*. Maratse wrestled his lips around the title, and then read the subtitle: *Volume 2*. He laughed again, flicked through the pages, and found Petra's note, her phone number, and a tight sprawl of words that he decided he would read later. Once he had finished his cigarette he passed through the airport doors to find a seat.

He was halfway into the first chapter when they called his flight. Maratse found the ticket from his wallet and hobbled to the check-in desk. For the first time in his life, he was given priority boarding, but he refused help to climb the steps at the back of the de Havilland Dash 7. He slumped down onto the grey faux-leather cushions of his seat and buckled the belt at his waist. The stewardess took his sticks to stow away. There was a wait while they finished loading the baggage and the other passengers boarded. Maratse pushed the tray table into position and lost himself in the book until the captain announced they were ready for take-off.

Maratse read until the last moment before take-off, when the thrust of the four turbo-prop engines pushed him back into his seat. He slipped Petra's note between the pages as a bookmark, and closed his eyes. He didn't open them again until they landed in Qaarsut, the gravel-strip airport on the Uummannaq peninsula.

He was the last to leave the aircraft, but the first to leave the airport. The gravedigger met him at the door.

"David Maratse?"

"*Iiji*," Maratse said, and shook the man's hand.

"I'm Karl Nielsen. I'm going to take you to Inussuk."

"On that?" Maratse said, and nodded at the quad bike parked behind Karl.

"*Naamik*, that's just to get down to the beach. I have a boat."

Maratse raised his eyebrows and smiled. He handed Karl his book as he climbed onto the quad bike. Maratse rested his sticks across his lap.

"Is this all you have?" Karl said and handed the book back to Maratse.

"It's all I need," he said.

Karl shrugged and shuffled into position, started the engine and clicked the bike into gear. Maratse flinched as they lurched forwards. He grabbed Karl's waist and held on as they raced down to the beach.

The icebergs in the bay were the size of villages. They reminded Maratse of the bergs in Ittoqqortoormiit, the place he used to call home. Karl slowed as they approached the beach, and Maratse smiled at the brown and bloody stains streaking the side of the small fibreglass dinghy at the water's edge. Karl waited for Maratse to get off, parked the quad beside the sledges and fishing boxes above the high water mark, and walked down to boat. He lit a cigarette as he walked and offered another to Maratse. Karl pushed the boat into the water and helped Maratse over the side. He pushed it further until the boat bobbed and the stern was deep enough that Karl could lower the propeller shaft and start the outboard motor. The fumes from the four-stroke engine tickled Maratse's nostrils and he drank it in, along with the smoke from his cigarette and the crisp air of autumn in the north.

"This is home," he whispered, before gripping the sides of the boat as Karl increased the throttle and they powered in a north-westerly direction along the peninsula towards Inussuk.

Chapter 6

The tide was out when Maratse arrived at his new home. Karl powered the fibreglass dinghy up the beach, cut the engine, and lifted the propeller shaft clear of the water and the lumps of ice in the shallow surf. He climbed over the side and helped Maratse out of the dinghy. Maratse took a deep breath and caught the whiff of dried fish lingering between the houses, salt and seaweed exposed on the rocks, together with a variety of cooking smells. Karl picked up Maratse's book, touched his elbow and pointed up the beach in the direction of the general store.

"Your house is over there. The dark blue one between the store, and the green house to the right."

"Who lives in the green house?"

"At the moment? A lesbian couple and their daughter." Karl waited for Maratse to react, and, when he didn't, he shrugged and said, "Follow me."

The shingle and coarse sand frustrated Maratse as he made his way from the boat to the steps of his new home. Karl waited and watched, but offered no help, for which Maratse was grateful. Visions of the rusty bar in the workshop flashed through Maratse's mind. He gritted his teeth and kept going. Just a few metres from the steps, a sledge dog puppy, barely three months old, toppled Maratse onto the beach as it slalomed between his sticks and legs. Maratse cursed and threw a small rock in the direction of the puppy, and it skittered after it as if it was a ball, biting at it with spiny teeth. Karl laughed when the puppy spat out the rock and bounced back to within a metre of Maratse.

Maratse held out his hand to Karl, and said,

"Give me a lift up." He clasped the gravedigger's hand and pushed off the beach as Karl helped him onto his feet. The puppy flopped onto its belly, rested its head on its legs and stared at Maratse. "Who's is it?" he asked.

"Nikki, my son's," said Karl. "Do you want it?"

"No," Maratse said, as he hobbled the last few metres to the steps of the house. He tucked his sticks under his arm and pulled himself up the steps with the thick wooden railings on either side. Karl opened the door and the puppy bounced up the steps and skittered around the deck. Maratse ignored it and followed Karl inside the house.

"There's no key," Karl said, as he kicked off his shoes and walked from the tiny hall into the living room, "and it smells like fish." The sofa separated the kitchen from the living area, and Karl pointed out the electric stove, fridge and kettle. He opened a cupboard and pointed at a selection of cups and glasses, plates and bowls. Maratse nodded and flopped onto the sofa. Karl placed Maratse's book on the coffee table and walked to the door. "My wife has made dinner for you. Come when you're hungry. It's the yellow house on the other side of the store."

"*Qujanaq*," Maratse said. He moved his sticks to one side as Karl pushed his feet inside his shoes.

"There's no TV," he said.

Maratse pointed at the book, and said, "I'll be fine."

"But there's a phone over there, by the window." He opened the door and kicked at the puppy as it tried to come in. He turned, and said, "Are you sure you don't want it?"

"Sure."

"Okay." Karl waved. "Yellow house," he said, and closed the door behind him.

Maratse heard Karl clump down the four steps to the beach, and then closed his eyes. The smell of fish lingered. Maratse rubbed at his nose, yawned and opened his eyes. The walls were patched with shadows of picture frames, the white window sills flecked with brown spots of fly shit, and the floor was gritty beneath his feet. Maratse grunted as he removed his boots. He leaned back on the sofa and patted his jacket pocket. He pulled out the packet of cigarettes, tipped the last two into his hand, and stuck one of them between his teeth. He found his lighter, and then stuffed it back in his pocket. Maratse closed his eyes for a second, reached for his sticks, and pushed himself onto his feet. He staggered to the door, opened it, and stepped out onto the deck. The puppy lifted its head, watching Maratse as he crossed the deck to the railing, leaned against it, and lit his cigarette.

"*Eeqqi,*" he said, as the puppy belly-crawled towards him. He lifted his finger and the puppy stopped. Despite himself, Maratse studied the pup's large paws, the shape of its head, and its bright brown eyes. It was mostly white with a grey mask, accentuated with white fur flaring to both sides of its muzzle. Maratse pictured the puppy in the winter, when its tail had dropped, and it was ready for harness. He grunted, finished his cigarette, and shuffled back inside the house. The telephone rang as he shut the door.

"Maratse," he said, as he lifted the receiver and answered the call.

"It's Petra. I found your number."

"*Iiji.*"

"Are you settling in?"

"I just arrived."

"I know. I just thought…"

Maratse watched the puppy through the window, as it curled into a ball outside the door. "How is the case?" he asked.

"Developing. We contacted the girl's friend in Aasiaat. It turns out they made a deal that Kaka would say Tinka stayed with her, but she was actually with a man."

"Man?"

"Yes. Older."

"Tinka is the missing girl?"

"Yes. Nivi Winther's daughter."

"The politician?"

"Yes." Petra paused. "You're interested, aren't you?"

"*Eeqqi,*" Maratse said. "Just making conversation."

"How's the book?"

"Difficult, but good."

"I'm sorry. There was nothing else."

"I like it. Thank you, Piitalaat." Maratse felt the pain burning through the nerves in his legs. He turned to look at the sofa. "I have to go," he said.

"That's okay. Can I call again?"

"*Iiji.* You can tell me about the case."

"I'll keep you posted. Enjoy your first night in your new home."

"I will." Maratse ended the call, frowning as he realised he had no bedding to speak of, and the bedroom was up a flight of steep stairs. He looked at the sofa again, and grabbed his sticks. *If I sit down, I won't get up again.* Maratse's stomach growled. He shuffled over to his boots, grimaced as he pressed his feet inside them, and then walked to the door, the ends of the laces tapping softly with each step. He opened the door, making the puppy slide along the deck.

Navigating the steps was more difficult on the way down, and complicated by the puppy weaving up and down between Maratse's legs. He stumbled and fell at the bottom when the puppy pounced on Maratse's laces. It recoiled several metres at the string of curses Maratse hurled at it, and further still as Maratse swore at each stage of getting to his feet. The ends of the sticks dug into the soft surface of the beach, and Maratse's trousers and jacket were dusted with fine black sand and plastered with tiny shell fragments. He dusted himself off and took the first few steps towards Karl's house. The puppy appeared in front of him a second later. Maratse cursed, and it recoiled. He took a step, and, as the dance continued, Maratse became aware of the small audience of children creeping out from beneath the decks of their houses to watch his progress. The puppy only had eyes for Maratse, its over-sized paws leaving pad prints along the beach, alongside the round imprints from the tip of Maratse's sticks.

They passed the store, and Maratse began to anticipate the puppy's movements. It was only when he reached the steps of the house, that he realised his focus had been on the puppy at his feet, not the pain in his legs. He paused at the bottom of the steps, nodding at Karl as he opened the door.

"Everything all right?"

"*Iiji,*" Maratse said, tucking the sticks under his

arm and climbing the steps to the house.

"Puppy bothering you?"

Maratse raised his eyebrows, *yes*.

"I'll get Nikki to put it on a chain tomorrow." Karl stood to one side as Maratse leaned on the wall to remove his boots. He hung his jacket on a peg, and walked into the living room. The smell of musk-ox stew made his stomach growl, and he smiled at Karl's wife as she guided him to a chair at the head of the small dining table. The television was on, and the news anchor from *Qanorooq* was halfway through the story of the missing girl.

"She's from here," said Karl.

"Who?"

"The mother, Nivi Winther. She grew up in Inussuk," Karl's wife said. "I used to play with her, when she was a child. I'm Buuti."

Maratse shook her hand and sat down. He looked at the television as Petra appeared, reading a statement from the police. He smiled as he listened to her appealing for people to come forward if they had any information concerning the whereabouts of Tinka Winther. She looked good, brushing loose strands of hair behind her ear as the wind picked up outside the police station. The image cut to a pre-recorded tape of Nivi Winther at a press conference, and the voice of the news anchor saying that Greenland's First Minister was not available to comment. Karl turned down the volume at a word from Buuti, as she served a generous helping of rice and stew on Maratse's plate. The thick dark sauce sank through the grains of rice and Maratse felt his stomach rumble at the sight of traditional Greenlandic food.

"I shot that one," Karl said. "On Svartenhuk."

"To the north?"

"*Aap*," he said, and nodded. "There's a small herd. But healthy. There's trout up there too. We can go this winter." Karl paused and glanced at Maratse's legs.

"I'd like that," Maratse said, and started to eat.

Buuti fussed over Maratse with another helping, followed by coffee and mint chocolate cake for dessert. The coffee settled the rich food in his stomach, and Maratse gestured that they go outside for a smoke. Karl followed him to the deck surrounding the house as Buuti cleared the table. The puppy lay on the beach below the house, pricking its ears as Maratse stepped onto the deck. It stood up, only to flop down again at a single word from Karl.

"Did you have dogs in Ittoqqortoormiit?" he asked.

"*Iiji*," Maratse said. "I had dogs."

"Do you miss it?"

"The dogs?"

"Being a policeman."

Maratse smoked for a moment before answering. He listened to the sea surfing gently up the beach, imagining the crackle and pop of air escaping from the clumps of ice in the water. He looked at the rock face on each side of the settlement, the wooden jetty stretching out from the concrete harbour, and the path zigzagging up the mountain knoll towering above Inussuk on the right. He could just see the radio mast and antenna. Karl's question hung in the air between them, unanswered. Maratse coughed, and picked a fleck of meat from his teeth.

"I do," he said. "But I am not a policeman anymore."

"What happened?"

"Lots of things," Maratse said, and an image of the Chinese man appeared before him, along with the smell, and the sound of the generator as it chugged with the effort of torture.

"I understand," Karl said. "I won't ask again."

Maratse nodded, finished his cigarette, and stubbed it out in an upturned plant pot. Buuti walked onto the deck with a pile of sheets in her arms. She pressed them into Maratse's arms and nodded in the direction of his house.

"You can use these until you get some of your own. There's a duvet and pillow upstairs," she said. Maratse caught her looking at his legs, and he smiled.

"I'll sleep on the sofa tonight," he said.

Buuti nodded, wished him a good night and disappeared inside the house. Karl finished his cigarette and offered to carry the sheets over to the house.

"I'll manage," Maratse said. He shook Karl's hand, tucked the sheets inside his jacket, and grabbed his sticks. The puppy was waiting for him at the bottom of the steps.

Maratse didn't fall on the walk back along the beach. But neither did he notice the children, or the fishermen waving from the dinghy just beyond the surf. Maratse was focussed on the puppy, and not falling on top of it. He let it bound up the steps in front of him, brushing it to one side with his stick as he opened the door.

The fish smell caught in his nose as he removed his boots. It was stronger than the smell of fish drying on the racks. He tossed the sheets on the sofa and walked into the kitchen. Maratse opened the fridge, and wrinkled his nose at the sight of a fillet of halibut sealed in a plastic bag. He took it out, closed the fridge door, and carried the fish to the deck. Maratse opened the bag and spilled the fish onto the deck in front of the puppy. The puppy seized the prize between its sharp milk teeth and scampered down the steps to tear into the fish on the beach. Maratse tossed the bag in the rubbish bin attached to the railing, closed the door and walked to the sofa. He sat down, let his sticks slide to the floor, and lifted his legs so that he could stretch on the sofa. Maratse reached for his book and propped it on his chest.

Soft cries and shouts carried on the wind as the children of Inussuk chased each other beneath the decks of the houses. Sledge dogs howled, and, if he hadn't been concentrating on the book, Maratse would have heard dog chains rattling across the rocks as they moved, the clap of a rubbish bin lid as Buuti got rid of the kitchen waste, and the occasional burr of a fishing dinghy as it motored past the rocks sheltering the beach.

The sirens of Nuuk were gone, as were the sounds of refuse trucks, a stream of traffic, shouts of greeting and drunken arguments on the steps outside the supermarket. The buzz of movement was gone, only the feet of the children, and the pads of the puppies on the beach remained. Maratse sank further into the sofa. He forgot about his legs, forgot about the Chinese man, and had no thoughts for the missing girl, not yet. He picked up his book and started the process of adjusting to his new life. There were no shifts, no paperwork, not even the chatter and static of the police radio. All he had left was his jacket, stained and patched as it was. He didn't think to remove it. On his first night in Inussuk, he didn't think at all.

Sisamanngorneq

THURSDAY

Chapter 7

Aarni Aviki parked next to Malik's huge Dodge RAM and walked up to the door. He let himself in and kicked off his shoes. Malik handed him a mug of coffee and nodded at the kitchen table.

"Let's sit over there," he said, and sat down by the window.

Aarni put his mug down on the table and opened his briefcase. Malik watched him as he pulled out a copy of *Sermitsiaq*. He dropped the newspaper on the table and sat down. "I take it you've read the article online?"

Malik nodded, and pulled the newspaper closer to him. "This is the girl?" he said, and tapped the photo on the front page. "Nivi Winther's daughter?"

"Yes." Aarni took a sip of coffee. "Her name is Tinka. She's seventeen." Aarni waited as Malik read the article, anticipating his reaction when he reached the penultimate paragraph. "Last seen with a middle-aged man at a party."

Malik turned the first page of the newspaper and pinched his chin. He was silent for a moment, and then said, "How bad is this?"

"That depends."

"On what?"

"Do you recognise her?"

Malik nodded.

"Are you that man?"

"Probably," Malik said. "Was I the last man? I don't know. She was pretty drunk." Malik rubbed his eyes, shook his head and took a long, slow breath. "She really is Nivi's daughter?"

"You know that." Aarni put down his coffee and

leaned back in his chair.

Malik looked out the window and started to speak. "Sipu comes home tonight. He has been away at football camp. That means I have to find somewhere to sleep." He looked at Aarni. "Naala won't have me in our bed." He nodded in the direction of the living room. "The sofa is too small." Malik sighed, and continued, "Pipaluk's grades have improved, including mathematics."

"That's good."

"It's good?" Malik said and laughed. "It's embarrassing. She is lousy at maths. Not particularly good at languages either. The teachers are grading her according to my popularity."

"Which is soaring," Aarni said, and reached into his briefcase. He pulled out a copy of the polls from the previous month, pointing at the annotations in pencil in the margins. "This was August. Projections have you much higher in October. But, you can expect to slip a little, because of this."

"Because I slept with the girl?" Malik said. He leaned forwards, reaching for the newspaper.

"Because she is missing. No-one knows you slept with her. This is a sympathy response. Nivi will get a spike in support, but it won't last. You have the popular vote."

"Until they find out I was that man."

"They won't."

"When they find the girl, they will. It's just a matter of time."

"No it isn't." Aarni said and shrugged. "It's taken care of."

"Taken care of?"

"It's done."

"What is done? What are you talking about?"

"I told you I was loyal, and now I need you to trust me."

Malik shook his head. "I don't understand. What exactly have you done?"

"*I* have done nothing. I'm just saying that you don't have to worry about the girl recognising you."

"Huh," Malik said. He took a sip of coffee, and stared at his communications chief over the lip of the mug. "What about the reporter? Is it the same one?" Malik peeled back the front page of the newspaper. "Qitu Kalia?"

"I presume so," Aarni said. He looked at his watch. "We agreed you would work at home today. You need to prepare for the debate. I have the notes in my briefcase."

"You think it's necessary? You don't think she'll cancel?"

"That's my next meeting." Aarni placed a sheaf of papers in a folder in front of Malik. "I am meeting with Daniel Tukku."

"Nivi's assistant."

"I think he likes to be called Chief of Staff, even though she doesn't." Aarni laughed. "I like to needle him about that." He stood up. "Don't answer any calls. Okay?"

"You said no-one knows. You said I shouldn't worry about it."

"But the smart move is to be unavailable. You don't need to comment on the opposition leader's poor parenting skills. I mean, she doesn't know where her daughter is."

"That's harsh, Aarni. I thought I was the cynical one."

"It doesn't matter. You have a perfectly good excuse – preparing for the debate – use it. Any comments from you might be twisted, and then there's the chance of you saying something unfortunate. We don't want that. This is the time when she can leap ahead of you. And, if the girl is found…"

"If?"

"Yes," Aarni shrugged. "No-one knows where she is. She might be in Denmark for all we know." Aarni looked at Malik and frowned. "What's wrong?"

"I was thinking of Pipaluk. How I would feel if she was missing."

"Well, she's not. Stop thinking about that." Aarni gestured at the notes. "Concentrate on the debate." He looked at his watch. "I have to go."

Aarni left Malik with the notes and the newspaper. He backed his car out of the drive and continued into the centre of town, parking at the rear of Hotel Hans Egede. He found Nivi's assistant waiting in the lobby café. The cut of the man's suit suggested it was expensive. Aarni tugged at the fit of his own suit, as the top button strained at the end of a short length of cotton. He unbuttoned his jacket, shook Daniel's hand, and sat down.

"Do you want something to drink?" Daniel asked in Greenlandic. "I could do with another latté."

"Sounds good." Aarni fiddled with the contents of his briefcase. He pulled out a single sheet of bullet points and placed it on the table between them. "They are in Danish. I thought the meeting could be in Danish."

Daniel laughed. "Of course." He twisted in his seat and ordered two lattés. He switched to Danish, and said, "Politics aside, I have been impressed with the way you have handled the press. They have been merciless."

"Thank you." The waiter brought their coffee. Aarni unwrapped the Italian biscuit placed by the side of the glass, dipping it in the frothed milk at the top. "It has been a challenge, but if they focus on the language…"

"You don't have to answer to anything else," Daniel said. "Yes, very smart."

"I thought so," Aarni said, and ate the biscuit.

"And what about Malik Uutaaq? Was it his strategy?"

"Mine." Aarni brushed biscuit crumbs from his lips. "And I don't mind admitting it."

"It's certainly working. I have to give you credit for that." He paused for a moment, studying his counterpart as he spooned the frothed milk from the lip of the glass. "Is this a candid meeting? I mean, can we be candid with one another, off the record?"

"I don't see why not," Aarni said. The spoon clinked against the glass as he placed it on the saucer. "Are you thinking about the debate?"

"The debate, policy, the polls. Although, we have been sidetracked this morning. You've seen the news?"

"Tinka Winther?"

"Yes."

"It's a real shame. Nivi must be quite distracted." Aarni nodded at the paper on the table. "Do you want to postpone the debate?"

"Today is Thursday. The debate is scheduled for Sunday night. I imagine this will be cleared up by then. Greenland is a small place after all."

"The largest small place in the world."

"Of course, but where can she go? If she hasn't drowned, that is." Daniel caught Aarni's eye as he reached for his latté. "She will turn up, I am sure."

"Well, we certainly hope so. Please pass on our sympathies to Nivi."

"I will." Daniel put his coffee on the table. "There is another matter I would like to discuss, before we get into the nitty gritty of the debate." Aarni waited as Daniel tugged a piece of paper from a folder tucked between him and the arm of his chair. He showed it to Aarni, and said, "It's a photocopy of a recent article in *Politiken*. You might have seen it."

"No," Aarni said. "It's new to me." He plucked the paper from Daniel's hand and pretended to skim read it.

"It's about the party culture of Greenlandic politics. It's a salacious read, more suited to American and British politics, but no less interesting."

"Why are you showing this to me?" Aarni laid the paper on top of the debate notes.

"You said we could be candid?"

"I did."

"Then what would your boss think of such an article? Would he say there was an element of truth to the story?"

"You would have to ask him."

"Yes, but I am asking you."

Daniel laced his fingers in his lap and waited, as Aarni made a show of stirring the remaining froth of steamed milk into his latté. The waiter visited their table and asked if they needed anything else.

"What do you want, Daniel?" Aarni asked, once the waiter had moved away.

"I want you to change the narrative. Stop talking about language, and start talking about housing, unemployment. Engage us on the grounds of governing, and there will be no need to talk about anything as sordid as booze and bad behaviour."

"And if we don't?"

"Then I see no reason why we can't circulate a story about the inappropriate desires and actions of married party leaders in the media. Do you?"

"Qitu Kalia."

"I'm sorry. What did you say?"

"Qitu Kalia. That's the name of your journalist."

"Possibly."

"Of course it is," Aarni said, and sighed. "I thought dirty campaigns were reserved for the American elections and Hollywood."

"Ah, Aarni, it's all about the news cycle, even here, especially here. For the voters outside of Nuuk," Daniel said, counting the larger Greenlandic towns on his fingers, "Sisimiut, Maniitsoq, Ilulissat and Qaqortoq, items of news tend to have a long shelf-life. And May is not so very far away, when you think about it. And what will your voters think about during the long, hard winter in the north, on the east coast, and even south of here? Do you really think your candidate can afford to lose popularity? It is the popular vote that is keeping him in the game."

"Ahead of the game," Aarni said. "As Nivi Winther's *assistant* I thought you would be more aware of her position in the polls." Aarni leaned forwards. "Behind Malik Uutaaq."

"And yet," Daniel said, the beginnings of a sly grin twitching at the corners of his mouth, "with this bump of sympathy, who knows what might happen. I mean, we all want Tinka to be found safe and sound, as soon as possible, but…"

"But?"

"If her body is found…" Daniel paused. "No matter how tragic the circumstances, that sympathy vote might just topple your lead."

Aarni swallowed as a bout of indigestion collected in his throat. He reached for the glass of coffee, and drained the last third with one gulp, aware of Daniel's eyes following his every move. He took a breath, placed the glass on the table, and leaned back in his chair, brushing at imaginary biscuit crumbs on his jacket.

"The sympathy vote," he said.

"Yes."

"That can go both ways." Aarni felt a renewed injection of confidence. He considered switching to Greenlandic, but decided not to push it. "In the event of such a tragedy, one might question how fit a grieving mother was to lead the country."

"There's that possibility."

"There is, and here is another. Who do you have in your party that could replace Nivi Winther, if she was forced to withdraw?"

"Forced? That's a strong word."

"Compelled is another. What if she was compelled to stand down, due to family matters?"

"Like the loss of her daughter."

"For example, yes. Who would take her place?"

In the silence that stretched across the low table between them, Aarni realised that Daniel had already considered the future implications of Tinka Winther's disappearance, and even her death. He appreciated in that moment, that Daniel was negotiating not on behalf of his leader, but himself. He allowed himself a smile over the text message he received earlier, confirming a loose end now secured. Then he tried to force the contents of his message as far from his mind as possible. He decided to wait for Daniel to speak. He didn't have to wait long.

"We have a number of suitable candidates."

"No you don't," Aarni said.

"We have one suitable candidate," Daniel said.

"Huh." Aarni tapped his fingers on his knee. "If I was to help you, by changing the narrative, what's in it for me? Because the minute I expose Malik Uutaaq to questions beyond language and identity ..."

"Is the very minute when we begin to campaign on an equal footing. That's all I ask. In the event that a change is necessary, it's all I can ask."

"This would be out of sympathy," Aarni said.

"I understand."

"And, in return, you will stop the publication of any salacious material that might implicate my boss?"

"I will."

Aarni took a long breath. "Well then, shall we discuss the questions for the debate?"

"I'm not sure that will be necessary. Nivi is far too preoccupied."

"Then you are going to cancel?"

"Oh, I wouldn't say that. I think we should continue regardless. It's important to show a strong leadership, even in times of duress, especially so, don't you think?"

"Then who will you send in her place?"

Daniel gestured lazily with his hand, and said, "We have a few possibilities, but, if necessary, I can always stand in for our leader. Just this once, you understand?"

"Oh, I think I understand," Aarni said. "Perfectly."

Daniel stood up, fastened the top button of his jacket and slipped the folder into his briefcase. He nodded at the bar. "I've already paid, but feel free to have another coffee on my tab, if you want to stay and mull things over for a while. You've got a few busy days ahead of you if you are going to have your candidate ready by Sunday night. Good luck." He waved as he walked away from the table.

Aarni watched him leave. He glanced at the customers sitting at the tables by the window, and then beckoned to the waiter that he would like another drink.

"Another latté?"

"No," Aarni said in Danish, "I'll have whisky. A double."

It was going to be a long weekend.

Chapter 8

The tramp of boots up the steps and onto the deck, followed by a heavy knock on the door forced Maratse to open his eyes and start a new day in Inussuk. He lifted his legs over the side of the sofa and wiped the sleep from his eyes and the dried saliva from the corner of his mouth, as Karl opened the door and kicked off his rubber boots in the hall. Maratse could hardly see Karl's face for all the things he carried in his arms. Karl dumped the gear on the coffee table and wished Maratse a good morning.

"Coffee?" Karl said.

"I haven't got any."

"I have." Karl picked up the plastic bag that was laying on top of the pile of clothes and walked into the kitchen. "Get dressed," he said.

"Where are we going?"

"Fishing."

Maratse reached out to tug at the pile of clothes, separating warm layers from a tough quilted overall that was greasy to the touch. "I need a shower," he said.

"When you get back." Karl filled the kettle, spooning two heaps of instant coffee into two mugs, as the water boiled. Maratse began to dress, exchanging the layers of clothing on the pile for his own sweaty shirt and police jogging trousers. He lifted his legs into his overalls, pulling them slowly up to his knees. "Need help?" Karl asked, as he put the mugs of coffee on the table in front of the sofa.

"*Iiji.*" Maratse pushed himself into a standing position. He held onto Karl's shoulder with one hand and pulled the overalls into position with the other.

"Where are we going?"

"I have a long fishing line running deep from the coast just north of Inussuk. I want to check it."

"Okay."

"I can show you a couple of good places along the way. For your own line."

"I need a boat."

"Edvard has a boat he wants to sell."

"And fishing line, gear?"

"I have enough for both of us."

Karl walked to the window and tapped the glass with his cracked thumbnail and smiled as the puppy lifted its head.

"It's been there all night," Maratse said.

"And been sick on the steps."

"That would be the fish." Maratse zipped the overalls to the collar and then back down to the waist. "I need to pee," he said.

"Edvard empties the buckets twice a week, but you'll have to register with the council."

Maratse nodded. "So, I have to register before I can pee?"

"Yes," Karl said and laughed, and then, "Pee outside, before we get in the boat." He handed Maratse a coffee, and pulled a packet of biscuits from the deep pocket of his overalls.

"What else do you have?" Maratse asked, as he took a handful of biscuits.

"Coffee and cigarettes."

Maratse grunted, dunked the biscuits in the coffee, and ate as Karl leaned against the window. The temptation to sit down nagged at Maratse, but he decided that now he was up he should stay up. He gauged the distance to the hall, looked for his sticks, and then decided to shuffle to the door without them. He put the mug down on the table and moved his right leg. A burst of pain streaked down his leg only to disappear a second later. Maratse gritted his teeth and ignored the pain in his legs, as he worked his way to the hall, shaking his head as Karl offered to help.

"Your boots are the ones with orange caps," Karl said, as Maratse rested against the door.

Maratse nodded, placed his hand against the door and grabbed a fistful of overall, lifting his leg and pushing his foot into the rubber boot. He rested for a second and then pushed his other foot into the second boot.

"Ready?" Karl asked, as he pulled on his own boots.

"*Iiji*," Maratse said and opened the door. The puppy bounded to its feet and nearly pushed Maratse off balance. He growled a quick command and the puppy retreated. Karl laughed as he closed the door behind them. "I used to have dogs," Maratse said.

"You will again," Karl said. "Starting with that one."

"We'll see."

Maratse used the railings to climb down each of the four steps to his house. He moved slowly, deliberately, and, when both his feet were on the beach, he shuffled towards the waterline, and Karl's dinghy, which was tethered through the eye of a large rusty piece of iron drilled into a boulder on the beach. The puppy danced just half a metre in front of Maratse, all the way to the dinghy, acting as the carrot leading the way, as well as the role of the stick that could trip Maratse onto the beach. If he had thought about it, Maratse might have given the puppy some credit for encouraging him to walk without help. But Maratse was preoccupied with reaching the dinghy. Once there he leaned against the gunwales, lowered his hand, whistled once, and made a fuss of the puppy as it bounded towards him. The puppy's soft fur tickling the coarse skin of Maratse's hand made him smile, and he thought about other dogs and teams that he had run on the east coast, before he met Konstabel Fenna Brongaard, before the Chinese man.

Maratse looked along the beach and waved at the fishermen preparing their gear, fixing lines, and stripping outboards. Just four men and not one of them younger than Karl. All of them were at least ten or fifteen years older than Maratse.

"Where are the young men?"

"At school, or in town," Karl said and waved in the direction of Uummannaq. "Inussuk is dying," he said. "We get a little trade each summer, when the cruise ships send passengers in to visit and buy cakes, and try Greenlandic food. But people are leaving Inussuk. One day it will be no more."

Maratse waved at the fishermen one more time and then shooed the puppy away. He used the gunwale to push himself to his feet as Karl pushed the dinghy down the beach and into the water. Maratse shuffled in his wake, following the shallow trench in the sand from the dinghy's hull. The sea lapped at his boots, as he clambered over the gunwales. Karl grabbed his arm and helped him onto the seat spanning the centre of the dinghy. Maratse zipped the overall to the collar and watched the puppy fret at the water's edge, as Karl lowered the outboard motor, pumped fuel from the plastic petrol can into the engine, and pulled the starter handle.

Maratse felt the weight of the boat shift as Karl sat down, and again when he handed Maratse a lit cigarette. Maratse rolled it into the gap between his teeth, tugged the collar of the overalls around his neck, and puffed a cloud of smoke into the wind, as Karl increased the throttle and they motored along the coast. Small clumps of ice skidded against the hull, thumping along each side until they were clear of the debris field from a small iceberg calving close to shore.

Karl slowed at various points along the way to his long line, pointing out rocks that were good for attaching one end of the line, high water marks, and the spots that he had used to place stone traps to catch Arctic foxes.

"Buuti cleans the pelts," he said, "and then sells them to the tourists."

"Are they allowed to buy them?"

"Maybe?" Karl said, and shrugged. "We don't ask, and neither do they."

Karl slowed as they neared a point on the peninsula that opened into a large bay. He steered the dinghy at a right angle to the point, and tapped Maratse on the shoulder. A large cube of polystyrene, with a faded flag pressed through the centre bobbed a hundred metres in front of them. Karl let the motor idle, and then clicked it out of gear. He cut the motor a second later and they drifted onto the fishing marker. Karl snagged the thick rope attached to a plastic buoy, hidden behind the marker, and tied a line from the dinghy through the buoy. He sat down and tapped Maratse on the back, gesturing for him to turn around.

"Coffee," Karl said, as he pulled a thermos flask

from the satchel at his feet.

"*Iiji*," Maratse said, and grinned. "You think of everything."

"I think of the essentials," Karl said, and handed Maratse a packet of cigarettes.

"You've been generous."

Karl shrugged. "You're my neighbour. You can bring cigarettes next time."

Maratse nodded and leaned forwards to reach the flame from Karl's lighter. For the next ten minutes they didn't speak, just enjoyed bobbing in the swell of the water, their eyes cruising the surface of the sea in anticipation of a seal coming up for air. Maratse cast a glance at the ropes and gear strewn about the dinghy, spotted the rusted barrel of the Sako .22 and smiled. Karl patted the breast pocket of his overalls and lifted the flap to reveal a plastic box of ammunition.

The trick, Maratse knew, was to startle the seal with the first shot, pushing it back under the water with little or no air in its lungs, while speeding towards its last location, and then firing again, and again, until the hunter could shoot the seal in the head, or the eye, and hook it with a gaff on a stick before the seal sank. The seal would supply meat for Karl's family for a few weeks, and the skin, depending on the time of year, could be sold for a little money, or sewn into gloves or a smock to be sold to the tourists for a lot more. The blubber was for the dogs over the winter, and the bones were a treat for the pack as soon as the carcass was stripped of everything else.

Maratse caught himself salivating at the thought of seal meat on the bone, sizzling in its own fat on a flat rock on the mountainside, with a fire of twigs and driftwood beneath it.

"Ready?" Karl asked, as he stood up. He placed his hand on Maratse's shoulder as he clambered over the centre seat and lifted a wooden stand from the bow of the dinghy. He slotted the base of the stand into two rectangular holes made of fibreglass fixed in position at the bow of the boat. Karl lifted a wooden wheel of fishing line into position. A length of wire with a metal clasp was tucked into a cut in the wood. Karl took it and reached over the gunwales for the fishing marker. He lifted the marker, snapped the clasp onto another clasp attached to the bottom of the flag, and released the marker, letting it bob at the end of a short line attached to the buoy. Karl straightened and slapped his hand on the wheel. "You or me?"

"Me," Maratse said, and prepared to move to the bow of the boat. He waited until Karl sat down on the stern seat. Maratse gritted his teeth and moved forwards, kneeling on two coils of rope in front of the wheel. He gripped the handles on both sides and began to turn. Behind him, Karl pulled a shallow plastic box from beneath the centre seat. He placed it in front of him and hooked the gaff around the fishing line as Maratse reeled it in from the depths of the sea. The boat turned and Karl let the line glide through the rubber glove he was wearing. When the first flat halibut broke the surface, Karl called for Maratse to stop, as he unhooked the fish and tossed it into the plastic box at his feet.

They continued like this for another five minutes, and seven fish, until the handles slipped out of Maratse's hands. The line started to sink back into the sea. Maratse stood up, ignoring the pain in his legs, gripped the handles and slowed the unravelling of the line. He grunted at the weight of the line as he began to turn the handles. He stopped to unzip his jacket with one hand, the fishing line trembled through the handle and into the palm of his other hand. The abrasions in the creases of his palms from the rusted bar of the ambulance workshop opened, and a smear of blood coated the handles as Maratse sweated with the weight.

"A shark, maybe?" Karl said. He peered over the side of the dinghy, as Maratse turned the handles, one slow revolution after another.

"Can you see it?" Maratse said during another pause.

"I can see something." The dinghy dipped to the port side as Karl gripped the fishing line and tugged at it. "Just a little more, and I can get it with the gaff." Maratse turned the wheel another three full turns until he heard Karl gasp.

"Can you see it now?" Maratse waited for a response, but Karl said nothing. He found a length of rope with a loop at one end. It was attached to the legs of the fishing wheel, and Maratse hooked the loop around the opposite handle, locking the wheel in position. He turned around as Karl retched over the side, spilling the coffee from his guts into the water. Maratse stared beyond the contents of Karl's stomach floating on the surface, and saw the slow twists and curls of long black hair moving in the water with the current.

"Do you have a mobile, Karl?"

"Yes," Karl said and tugged his mobile from his pocket. He handed it to Maratse and then moved along the stern seat to the starboard side of the dinghy.

Maratse crawled over the centre seat, ignoring the trim of the boat as he leaned over the side and stared into the glacial white face of a dead girl at the end of the line. He reached into the water and turned her head upwards. The eyes were gone, and the girl's skull felt soft on one side. She was young, Maratse reckoned, and dressed in winter clothes, which was strange, he realised, as the body was well-preserved and perhaps only a week or two old. Despite the damage, she looked familiar, and he remembered the photo he had seen on the news the night before. He let go of the girl's head, and worked his way onto the centre seat.

"Karl?" he said. "Have a cigarette." Karl nodded as Maratse unlocked the keypad on the mobile and dialled the police station in Nuuk.

Chapter 9

Petra noticed the Police Commissioner the minute he walked through the door and onto the first floor office area where she had her desk. He towered above the majority of the police officers in Nuuk. People said he was tall, even for a Dane. Petra was in her second year of training when Lars Andersen had been appointed Commissioner for the police in Greenland. Prior to his arrival, it was rumoured that he didn't tolerate fools or foolish behaviour. It was known that he had an impressive record for policing in Denmark, including a short period overseas, in Nicaragua. But it was a secret, between Petra and the Commissioner that he was mildly dyslexic. Cadets spent their second year of training at the police academy in Nuuk stationed around the country on a practical placement, under the supervision of a mentor. Petra had been in Nuuk, and had surprised the Commissioner one day when he was struggling to work his way through a pile of detailed reports. She offered to help, and he was impressed by the speed at which she read and her flare for Danish grammar.

As the Commissioner made his way along the floor towards her desk, she smiled at the memory of how grateful he had been for her help.

The Commissioner did not smile as he approached Petra's desk. He nodded hello and borrowed a chair from the adjacent desk, and sat down. He crossed one long leg over the other and said, "I need an update on the Tinka Winther case."

"Okay," Petra said, and flipped open her notebook. She scanned her notes and said, "The last person to see Tinka was her father, Martin Winther. I spoke to him yesterday. He said she was staying with a friend, Kaka Satorana, but the girl admitted it was a cover story."

"Covering for Tinka?"

"Yes, the truth was that Tinka was planning to go to a party. Kaka said Tinka was excited about meeting a particular man."

"Older?"

Petra nodded. "Kaka said the man was older, yes."

"Any leads on the man?"

"No, but…" Petra closed her notebook.

"But? You have a hunch?"

"Sort of." She opened the first drawer of her desk and placed a photocopy of a newspaper article on the desk in front of the Commissioner. "Someone left this on my desk last night."

"Give me the gist of it," the Commissioner said, his voice low as he studied the article.

"It's about the party culture of politicians in Greenland."

"A party culture?"

"Amongst some politicians, yes." Petra paused. "It is suggestive, but mentions no current names, only those from the past, before the millennium."

"And your hunch is that Tinka was meeting a politician?"

"I think that's why someone left this on my desk."

"Any idea who?"

"Who left the article?"

"Yes, or the politician. Your best guess."

Petra looked over the Commissioner's shoulders. Three of her colleagues were working at their desks, and a fourth police officer walked through the door with a report in one hand and a coffee in the other. Petra felt a twinge in her stomach.

"Petra?"

"Can we…" Petra started, and then nodded at the glass-walled meeting room to her left. She stood up and gestured for the Commissioner to follow her. Petra imagined a lull in the activity at her colleagues' desks, as she opened the door to the meeting room. She closed it behind the Commissioner, pressed her hands together, and tapped her lips with her fingertips.

"Well, now we have the attention of the entire office, Petra. Are you sure this is necessary? Bear in mind that this is Greenland, Constable, not Hollywood," the Commissioner said, and sat on the table. "However," he said, as he stretched his legs in front of him, "this is political, so you are probably right to be cautious."

"Thank you."

"Do you have a name?"

"I have a name, and a date, and a location."

The Commissioner raised his eyebrows. "Go on."

"It's all supposition, of course," Petra said. The Commissioner made a spinning gesture with his finger, and she continued. "Malik Uutaaq was in Ilulissat for a meeting last weekend. I confirmed this with his secretary."

"Tinka is a high school student in Aasiaat. Am I right?"

"She's a second year student. She has been sick, and was at home in Ilulissat with her father."

"So she was in Ilulissat at the same time as Malik Uutaaq."

"Yes."

"He's married, isn't he?" he said, and Petra nodded. The Commissioner stood up. "As evidence goes, that's pretty thin."

"I said it was a hunch, based on someone leaving the article on my desk."

"And who was that I wonder?"

"I have no idea."

"All right, if this develops, I think you should talk to Uutaaq's wife." The Commissioner sighed. He walked to the office window and looked out at the sea. The clouds were the same colour as the water, and swathes of rain were storming towards the land. "We have a meeting next door," he said, "in the government building. You and I are going to meet with Nivi Winther and her assistant. I think his name is Daniel."

"Tukku," Petra said.

"That's right. We're a little late, but I wanted to talk to you first." He walked to the door and opened it. "Oh, and I asked Gaba Alatak to meet us there."

"Why?" Petra said. She paused at the door as the twinge in her stomach developed into a queasy feeling.

"Because he is an impressive figure, leader of the Special Response Unit, and I want the minister to feel that we are putting our best people on this. That includes you, Constable."

"Yes, sir," Petra whispered, as she followed the Commissioner out of the meeting room and along the office floor to the stairs. "But did it have to be Gaba?"

"Am I missing something?" the Commissioner asked, as he strode down the stairs. Petra hurried to keep up, despite the feeling of lead in her stomach.

"We were dating," she said, "until he decided younger girls were more interesting."

"That seems to be popular at the moment."

"Yes, sir."

The Commissioner stopped to shake hands with a young police officer, newly returned from paternity leave. Petra waited as the proud father produced a photograph from his wallet. The Commissioner smiled, patted the man on the back, and wished him well. He beckoned to Petra and they walked out of the main door and into the rain.

"I've been meaning to ask you something," he said, as they jogged through the rain the short distance to the government offices. "How is Constable Maratse?" The Commissioner stopped at the door, opened it, and waited for Petra to go inside.

Petra smoothed the rain from her hair, then wiped her hands on her jacket and nodded. "He's okay, all things considered. He flew to Inussuk yesterday."

"Where's that?" the Commissioner asked as he led the way to the elevator.

"In Uummannaq fjord, just up the coast from Ilulissat."

"And what is he going to do?"

"He says he is going to fish and hunt," Petra said, as the elevator arrived. She paused before walking inside.

"You're not so sure, are you?"

"No, sir. He's in a lot of pain. According to the doctors, he suffered a lot of nerve damage when they tortured him."

"Constable," the Commissioner said quietly, as

the doors closed, "that is classified information. I told you because I needed someone to take care of Maratse."

"I know, sir."

"Then I expect us to talk about Maratse without mentioning what actually happened, especially inside this building."

"Yes, sir. Sorry, sir."

"So, we understand each other. Good. Now," he said, "compose yourself, I'm about to present you to the First Minister as one of Greenland's brightest police officers."

"Thank you," she said, and then, as the doors opened, she asked, "And Gaba?"

"Purely decoration. Unless we need the services of his team. He will have no say in the case. It's yours, and you report to me, directly."

"But I'm only a Constable," Petra said, as they walked out of the elevator and along the hall.

"Not anymore," the Commissioner said, as they stopped outside Nivi Winther's office. "Congratulations, Sergeant," he said and shook her hand. "Your results came in early this morning. The official papers will be on your desk by the end of the day." The Commissioner winked as he knocked on the door and opened it.

Petra's stomach wrestled with conflicting emotions, as she tried to process everything the Commissioner had told her since he sat down at her desk only a short while ago. She knew she had done well in the Sergeant's exam, but having things confirmed by the Commissioner made it suddenly real. Petra allowed herself a brief smile before entering the room. She glanced at Gaba looking impressive, and then at the First Minister. Nivi Winther had obviously decided not to wear make-up, and, at the sight of tears welling in her eyes, Petra believed the decision had been wise.

"This is Sergeant Jensen," the Commissioner said, and beckoned Petra towards the desk. She shook Nivi's hand, and nodded at her assistant, Daniel, as he stood behind the First Minister. "Petra handles missing person's cases, and, on this matter, she will be reporting to me directly."

"And him?" Daniel said with a nod towards Gaba.

"Gaba is here at my request. I want him to be fully informed in the event that we need him."

"Why would we need him?" said Nivi. "What does he do?"

Gaba took a step forwards. "I lead the Special Response Unit. If we find your daughter, we might need my team."

"If?" Nivi said. "I don't understand."

"This is a high-profile case, First Minister," said the Commissioner. "If we were in America, and the first daughter went missing, well, I think we can all imagine how they would react over there."

"And over here?" said Daniel.

"This is Greenland," the Commissioner said. "We don't have a precedent for such situations, but I want to assure you, that we are taking this seriously, and we are doing everything we can to find the First Minister's daughter."

"You are doing everything you can?"

"Yes, we are."

"Daniel, don't," said Nivi.

"It's all right, Nivi," he said. "I just want to be

sure that they really are doing everything they can. I want to know if you have any leads?"

"I can assure you that we are actively investigating Tinka's disappearance."

"And do you have any suspects?"

"Daniel," Nivi said, "stop."

He turned to Nivi, and said, "This is important. I have to ask."

"And I said I didn't want you to."

Petra watched as the First Minister fought to control her breathing. She looked at the Commissioner, opened her mouth to speak, and shut it again when he urged caution with a subtle wave of his hand.

"This is not about an article, Nivi, this is about your daughter." Daniel took a step towards her and placed his hand on her shoulder. He looked at the Commissioner. "What about Malik Uutaaq?"

"What about him?"

"There has been some suggestion that Tinka may have met Malik at a party, and that they may have…" He paused to squeeze Nivi's shoulder, mouthing the words I'm sorry. She nodded, and he continued, "They may have spent some time together. They may have been intimate."

The Commissioner nodded. He turned to look at his officers. Petra took a step forwards and he stood to one side, gesturing for her to approach the desk.

"Do you have a witness who can confirm that Malik Uutaaq was with your daughter, Ms Winther?" Petra waited as Nivi looked at Daniel.

"We know he was in Ilulissat at the same time as Tinka," he said.

"Yes, we have also confirmed that."

"Then you have spoken to Malik?" said Daniel.

"No."

Daniel let go of Nivi's shoulder and walked to the window and Gaba took a step back to give him room. The rain intensified, making it difficult to see the gentle curves of the Katuaq Cultural Centre, inspired as they were by the Northern Lights. Daniel looked at Petra. "Why not?"

"Being a man in Ilulissat does not make Malik Uutaaq a suspect. He is also a politician. If we questioned him without just cause, then we could make this situation worse."

"How could it possibly be worse?" Nivi said. "My daughter is missing. No-one has seen her since the weekend, perhaps as late as Friday night."

"I understand," Petra said, "but unless we have a witness, or some evidence linking your daughter and Malik Uutaaq, we risk creating a media storm, and you will be accused of using your daughter's disappearance to discredit a political opponent."

"That's quite the political insight, Sergeant," said Daniel. "Thank you. But when we want your political opinion we will ask you for it, not before. I suggest you concentrate on police duties, rather than your evident passion for political commentary."

Petra could feel her cheeks begin to redden, and looked at the Commissioner for support, but it was Gaba that defused the situation and put the First Minister's assistant firmly in his place.

"Sergeant Jensen is doing her job. She is considering all eventualities, and focussing on the one person she is accountable to in this investigation: Tinka Winther. I suggest you let her do her job, or provide her with the evidence necessary to pursue the line of inquiry you suggest." Gaba looked at Petra and gave her the briefest of smiles. He looked at Daniel and waited.

"Nivi?" Daniel said.

"Yes," she said and nodded.

"Thank you Sergeant Alatak. I can assure you I have every confidence in Sergeant Jensen's ability to conduct the investigation, and on that note, to further her lines of inquiry, as you so eloquently put it, might I suggest that she speak with Aarni Aviki, the Communications Chief for *Seqinnersoq.*" Daniel turned to Petra. "I think he will give you the necessary just cause to talk with Malik Uutaaq, without unleashing a political storm, although I do appreciate your concern."

"Thank you," Petra said. She looked at Nivi, intending to reassure her when her phone vibrated in her pocket. Nivi nodded that she should answer the call, and Petra swiped her thumb across the screen.

"Piitalaat," said Maratse, his words crackling in the wind, "I have found something."

Chapter 10

Malik Uutaaq turned on the television and surfed to the Teletext channel of Greenland's official television station, *Kalaallit Nunaata Radioa*. As the channel cycled through pages of brief text in Greenlandic and then Danish, he turned on the radio, checked his watch, and waited for the hourly news broadcast. Aarni said he should be prepared for some disturbing news, and that he was on his way over. Malik saw the Danish version of the news about a girl's body being found in Uummannaq fjord just before the hour. He turned on the radio and caught the presenter's last words about the girl, Nivi Winther's daughter, before the station switched to a telephone interview with the local Chief of Police in Uummannaq.

When he arrived, Aarni found Malik with his head in his hands, sitting on the edge of the sofa. The news broadcast was over, and so it seemed was Malik's interest in a political career.

"I'm pulling out," he said, as Aarni came into the living room.

"You can't. The country needs a strong leader. It should be you."

"A strong leader?" Malik looked up. "And what happens when someone tells the country that their leader was the last person to see Tinka Winther alive? Eh? What happens then?"

"It won't happen."

"You know, you say that every time, Aarni. I think you should explain yourself."

"All right," Aarni said. He walked into the hall and looked up the stairs. When he returned he closed the living room door. "We're alone?"

"Yeah," Malik said and stood up. "The kids are at school. Naala is at work."

"Turn off your phone."

"What?"

"Just turn it off," Aarni said. He found the landline in the kitchen, traced the lead to the wall, and pulled it out of the socket."

"What are you doing?"

"Precautions. That's all."

Aarni pushed an armchair closer to the coffee table and gestured for Malik to sit on the sofa. The shadow of a delivery van passed the window, and Aarni stood up to draw the blinds. Malik watched him as he walked back to the chair and sat down.

"What did you do?" Malik said.

"Just wait." Aarni took a breath and loosened the tie around his neck. He looked at Malik, and said, "This is all happening quickly. I'm trying to keep ahead of it, but you have to understand…"

"Just talk. Right now."

"Fine, okay." Aarni wiped his hand with his face. "All right. This is what happened. You went to Ilulissat as planned, last week."

"I came back Saturday afternoon."

"Right, after the party on Friday night. Where you met Tinka Winther."

"I didn't know it was her, Aarni, I swear."

"Sure, but you met her, and someone saw you with her. I know because I got a call around lunchtime on Saturday, before you landed in Nuuk."

Malik stood up and walked to the window. He leaned against the wall by the side of the blinds, and peered through the gap at the street. He tapped his fingers against his leg as Aarni talked.

"The call was from a man, but the line was distorted – but he spoke in Danish, good Danish."

"What did he want?"

"He said he could fix the problem, but it wouldn't be cheap."

"Aarni," Malik said, and looked at his communications chief, "did you pay someone to kill Tinka Winther?"

"No," Aarni said and shook his head. "No way." He pointed at Malik, and said, "*We* paid someone to fix your sexual indiscretions. That's what *we* did. That's all we did."

"You keep saying *we*, Aarni. Do you mean the party? Because I don't remember giving you any money to fix anything. And I will say that in court if I have to."

"You won't have to," Aarni said, his voice louder than he expected. He took a breath and spoke quietly, his words measured and spaced. "The party has attracted foreign interest. We had an injection of funds at the end of last week, and I used a portion of that to clean up your mess. *We*, the party, are in this together."

"When were you going to tell me about the investor?"

"I would have told you on Monday, but I was dealing with this," he said, and waved at the text page on the television. "I received a text when we drank coffee the other morning confirming that it was done. Fixed."

"Confirming that Tinka was dead?"

"No. I never expected it to come to that."

"Just what did you expect?"

"I don't know," Aarni said, aware once again that

he had raised his voice. "Money, maybe. A threat. Blackmail, perhaps. That's what I imagined. I didn't expect anything, other than the problem would go away, and that we could move on."

"And you didn't know it was Tinka Winther?"

"Okay, that I knew. That's what the man told me. That's why I had to fix this. The other girls," Aarni said, as Malik opened the drinks cabinet beside the television, "didn't matter. They were either too drunk or too stoned to remember who you were."

"You asked them?" Malik took two glasses and a bottle of gin from the cabinet. He put them on the coffee table and filled each glass to the brim. Aarni shook his head as Malik pushed the glass across the table with two fingers. Malik shrugged and drained both glasses.

"Yes, Malik, I asked them. I have cleaned up after all your indiscretions. I even talked with your wife."

"You did what?" Malik spluttered the last of the gin from his lips.

"I talked with Naala. We agreed you were a bastard. But we also agreed that you could be the next leader of Greenland, and that she could expect things to get better, financially, and at home. We agreed it was better for your kids that she put up with you screwing around, rather than dragging them through a messy divorce."

"You've been busy, Aarni." Malik reached for the bottle of gin, and then pushed it away. He collapsed against the cushions and leaned his head back over the back of the sofa. "And now I am chief suspect in a murder investigation."

"You don't know that."

"Come on, Aarni. It's just a matter of time."

Malik flicked his hand towards the television. "Your mystery guy will demand more money. That's how this works. Don't you watch television?"

Aarni leaned his elbow on the arm of the chair and rested his hand in his palm.

"There's more," said Malik, "isn't there?"

"Daniel Tukku knows you were with Tinka."

"What?" Malik lifted his head and stared at Aarni. "I thought you said we were going to be all right."

"I did, and we are."

"Not if Nivi Winther's assistant knows I was with her daughter we're not."

"We are, because I made a deal with him, yesterday."

"What deal?"

"I agreed that we would ease up on Greenlandic as the first language, and instead we would debate topics like housing and unemployment on Sunday."

"You really think the debate is still on? With everything that has happened? Nivi is in no position to debate. They will cancel. *I* would cancel if it was Pipaluk's body they dragged out of the sea." The thought of his daughter sobered Malik, and he pushed himself up and off the sofa. Without a word, he capped the gin bottle and put it back in the cabinet. He picked the glasses off the coffee table and took them into the kitchen. He filled the kettle and switched it on, hunting through the cupboard for two clean mugs until Aarni interrupted him.

"There will be a debate, and you will be there. I made a deal with Tukku that he would keep quiet in return for an open debate, one that allowed for other agendas than our own."

"You agreed to that?"

"Yes," Aarni said.

"Then you just lost the election for us. As soon as I go off message, I will be challenged on topics I haven't prepared."

"Maybe you would be prepared, if you spent less time screwing around."

Malik raised his finger, and then lowered it. "You're right," he said, and leaned against the kitchen counter. "I accept that. Anyway, Nivi is hardly likely to comment, if she even turns up."

"I don't think she will," Aarni said. He waited for a moment. "I think Daniel Tukku will stand in for her. I think he is ready to take advantage of the sympathy vote, and the potential vacuum this creates in the party. I think he plans to step in for Nivi on Sunday, and maybe in the future too."

"That's pretty heartless."

"No," Aarni said, "it's just politics." He took his keys out of his pocket and nodded at the kettle steaming by the side of the hob. "I don't want coffee. I'm going back to the office. Keep your phone turned off. I'll send you an email if I need to contact you."

"And what are you going to do?"

"I'm going to write a press release expressing our condolences to Nivi Winther and her family, and then I'm going to talk to Tukku, about the debate."

"Just like that?"

"Yes. It's business as usual, Malik. Remember that."

Aarni left the kitchen and walked out of the house. He shut the front door behind him and got into his car. The day was overcast like the one before it, but no rain. Aarni started the car and backed out of the drive. When he slowed at the first roundabout on his way into town, he noticed a police car in the mirror. Aarni accelerated, the tyres screeching into the bend as he turned onto the road leading up a small rise before dropping down a curve towards the centre of Nuuk. He glanced at the mirror again, increased speed, and gripped the wheel as the blue lights on the roof of the police car began to spin, followed by the blare of the siren.

The curve in the road was sharper than Aarni remembered. He struggled to negotiate the turn, overcompensating as the steering wheel grew heavy and slippery from his sweaty palms. The police car dropped back a little, as Aarni drifted into the opposite lane. The driver of the first car in a line of three heading towards Aarni braked, as Aarni clipped the side of the car with the bumper and screeched to a halt. He tried to open the driver's door but managed only a few centimetres before hitting the side panel of the other car. Aarni began to clamber over the handbrake to the passenger's side of his car, only to stop when the seatbelt locked, and a tall policeman peered through the glass of the passenger door. Aarni didn't recognise the face of Gaba Alatak. Gaba adjusted the arms of the Oakley sunglasses he wore around the back of his head. He knocked on the window, and gestured for Aarni to roll it down.

"That," Gaba said, as Aarni pressed the window button behind the handbrake, "was stupid."

"I know," Aarni said. He tried to shrug but the seatbelt tightened, forcing him back into his seat.

"You are Aarni Aviki?"

"Yes."

"I've been looking for you. Why don't you answer your phone?"

"I turned it off."

"Really?" Gaba said, and nodded. "Now, that's interesting. A communications chief with no means of communicating." He looked at the line of oncoming traffic, and glanced at his partner who was talking with the driver of the other vehicle. "How about we fix this mess, and then we can talk?"

"Yes," Aarni said. He watched as Gaba directed the traffic around the collision in the centre of the road. His partner took a statement from the driver of the other vehicle, stood back to take a few photos with his smartphone, and then waved the driver on. The man tapped on Aarni's window, told him to get out of the car. He drove the damaged car onto a patch of gravel by the side of a grill bar, while Gaba beckoned to Aarni to join him in the police car.

"Right," Gaba said, as Aarni climbed into the back of the Toyota and closed the rear passenger door, "that's sorted. We'll leave the rest to your insurance companies."

"Okay," Aarni said.

The second policeman opened the driver's door and got behind the wheel, nodding when Gaba told him to take them back to the station.

"I'm not the investigating officer," Gaba said, as his partner pulled out and away from the side of the road. "But before you meet her, I'd just like to tell you who I am." Gaba dipped his head and caught Aarni's eye. "I'm the guy they send in when the situation demands a more physical response. If you understand what I mean?"

"I'm not sure I do." Aarni's voice faltered as Gaba tilted his head and smirked.

Gaba turned to his partner, and said, "He doesn't

understand."

The policeman shook his head. "Better tell him straight, boss," he said.

"Really? You think a more direct approach would be better?"

"I do."

The policeman slowed at the entrance to the police station. He found a parking spot opposite the main entrance and turned off the engine. He waited as Gaba got out of the car, opened the rear passenger door, and slid onto the seat beside Aarni.

"My partner thinks I need to be more direct. So, how about we try this," he said, and prodded Aarni's chest with his knuckle. "I'm the one they send in to arrest people who have done unspeakable things." He lowered his knuckle as Aarni gasped for breath. "Arrests like that can be messy. It's not always easy to maintain control over a situation like that. Things can get out of hand quickly." He looked at Aarni. "People can get hurt."

"I think," Aarni said, his words stumbling out of his mouth, "I think I understand now."

"Good," Gaba said, and patted Aarni on the chest with a large, flat palm. "Just remember that, if you see me again. Okay?" Gaba got out of the car, opened Aarni's door, and escorted him inside the police station. Petra was waiting at the door.

"What was all that about?" she asked with a glance at Aarni.

"That?" Gaba said, and shrugged. "I don't know what you're talking about. What about you, Miki?" he said to his partner.

"Nope. No idea, boss." Miki turned to Petra, and said, "He's all yours."

Chapter 11

The hotel boat chartered by the Uummannaq police department dipped, as the Chief of Police, Torben Simonsen, and his assistant Constable Danielsen, heaved Tinka Winther's body over the railings and onto the deck. The girl's flesh sagged as water pooled out from her clothes, exiting her body from the open wound in her skull. Simonsen waved at Maratse, beckoning for him to come alongside. Karl started the outboard motor, and edged the dinghy along the hull of the hotel boat, until Maratse was positioned opposite the gap in the railings. Simonsen helped him onboard and Karl pulled away from the boat, searching for a comfortable distance between him and the dead girl.

"Constable," Simonsen said, as he waited for Maratse to find his balance. "We've never met, but we have a mutual acquaintance."

"We do?"

"Fenna Brongaard," he said with a nod towards Danielsen. "I don't like to admit it, but she pistol-whipped the two of us earlier in the year. Followed by a shoot-out in the old schoolhouse in Uummannatsiaq." Simonsen nodded to the tip of an island barely visible between the icebergs in the distance. He frowned at Maratse's grip on the railing and said, "Looks like I got off lightly."

"Hmm," Maratse said. He stifled a grimace and started walking along the railing towards the bow.

"You don't like to talk about it, Constable?"

"I'm not a Constable."

"Not anymore, maybe," Simonsen said, as he stood to one side of Maratse. They looked down at the body. "You know who she is?"

"*Iiji*," Maratse said. "Tinka Winther, the First Minister's daughter."

"Local politician. She's from Inussuk."

"I know." Maratse shuffled forwards, gritting his teeth as he knelt beside Tinka's body. He leaned over her head and pressed his face close to the open wound in her skull, then, working downwards, he examined the length of her body, without touching her.

"A boating accident would do that," Simonsen said, and tapped a cigarette from a packet into his hand. He offered one to Maratse.

"It could," he said, and rolled the unlit cigarette between the gap in his teeth. Maratse stared at the girl's clothes, peeled back the water-logged *Canada Goose* jacket and tugged at the fleece she wore beneath it. He used the railings to pull himself onto his feet, and said, "No underwear."

"No?"

"And her clothes are too small."

"The jacket fits," Simonsen said. He handed Maratse his lighter as he knelt beside the girl's head. There was a tag, just visible inside the hood, and he moved Tinka's head to read it. "Pipaluk Uutaaq," he said, and looked at Danielsen. "Write that down."

"Got it," Danielsen said, and flashed the page of his notebook at his chief.

"Uutaaq. Does the name mean anything to you? It seems familiar."

"The politician," Maratse said, as he remembered Petra's outburst at the article in the newspaper.

"Malik Uutaaq?"

"*Iiji.*"

Simonsen stood up, leaned against the railings, and tapped the ash from his cigarette into the sea. He looked at Maratse and took his lighter when Maratse was finished with it. "What do you think?" he asked.

"I'm not a policeman. I shouldn't say."

"You were, and I'm asking. You found her," Simonsen said, "and I found out your first call was to Nuuk, not to me." He stared at Maratse as he took a drag on his cigarette. "Would you mind telling me what's going on, *Constable*?"

Maratse stuck his hands in the pockets of the overalls and puffed a cloud of smoke from his lungs. He remembered telling Petra that he couldn't go back to Ittoqqortoormiit because he would always be a policeman, and would be treated as such. It seemed that moving to Inussuk had not changed anything. He was still a policeman, albeit unofficially. He flicked at the filter of the cigarette and shrugged.

"I called Petra Jensen."

"In Nuuk?"

"*Iiji.*"

"Why?"

"She is looking for a missing girl," Maratse said and dipped his head towards Tinka's body. "Her."

"And you are sure this is Tinka Winther?"

"It's the same girl from the news."

"Write that down too," Simonsen said with a nod at Danielsen. "It's curious that you are so sure it is her."

"I saw her on the news."

"So did I, but I don't recognise her." Simonsen took a last drag on his cigarette and flicked the butt into the water. "Lucky for us, and you, that Nivi Winther, is flying here tomorrow."

"Hmm."

"Constable Maratse," Simonsen said as he pushed away from the railings, "if you're going to live here and get involved in my investigations, I would appreciate you being more cooperative."

"I am cooperating."

"And going over my head."

"I explained that."

"You did." Simonsen tucked his hands into his belt. "But this is my jurisdiction. And, as you said, you're not with the police anymore. So," he said, and leaned forwards, "you might want to think about your priorities. Otherwise, I might be inspired to consider other aspects of this case."

"Such as?"

"How convenient it is that it was you that found the girl…"

"She's been dead for a few days."

Simonsen ignored Maratse, and continued "…on your very first day in Inussuk."

Maratse leaned against the railing, as the boat rose on the shallow crest of a wave. He stared at the Chief of Police through a cloud of cigarette smoke. "Is this really about me?"

"I don't want it to be," Simonsen said, "but you know as well as I do that investigations can take many turns before they are resolved."

"And you want to investigate me?" Maratse shook his head. "Because I called Nuuk first?"

"You have a mysterious past, Constable, with a lot of blank spaces that no-one seems to want to talk about. You were involved with a person of interest…"

"Fenna Brongaard…"

"That's right. From the little I heard, you might even have broken some laws in helping her."

"And that ties me to this girl?" Maratse said, with a nod towards the body on the deck. "That's pretty thin."

"And yet," Simonsen said, and smiled, "it's all I have right now."

"I think I should go." Maratse waved for Karl to come back.

"We can take you back to Inussuk. It's quite a drop into Karl's boat."

"I can manage."

"I'm sure you can." Simonsen waited as Maratse made his way along the railings. "Just remember our little chat, Constable. Remember your priorities."

"I will." Maratse nodded at Karl, as he clicked the outboard out of gear and bumped the side of the boat. He took a last look at Tinka's body before Danielsen covered it with a plastic tarpaulin. The driver of the hotel boat looked relieved when Maratse caught his eye.

Maratse lowered himself to the deck and lifted his legs over the side. As soon as he was seated Karl clicked the motor into reverse, and edged away from the hotel boat as Simonsen lit another cigarette.

"I'll call if I need you," he shouted.

Maratse held on to the seat, as Karl turned the dinghy in a tight arc and pointed the bow towards Inussuk. When the boat levelled out, he plucked the cigarette butt from his teeth and flicked it into the water. Karl was silent as they motored towards the settlement, turning once in a while to avoid growlers of ice, or to go around a large iceberg. The air was chill on Maratse's cheek, and he looked at the thick grey clouds above them, and imagined that the first snow of the year would soon fall. He said as much to Karl, but the older man just shrugged, focussing on getting home. Just ten minutes later he bumped the hull of the dinghy onto the beach.

"Leave the fish and the gear to me, I'll sort it," Karl said as Maratse tried to help. "Maybe we can talk later."

Maratse nodded and left him alone, shuffling up the beach as the puppy bounded towards him from where it was sleeping on the sand beneath the deck of Maratse's house. The Danish girl was playing in the sand. She said hello as he reached the steps. Maratse shooed the puppy from his feet and smiled.

"My name is Nanna," she said. "Mummy is inside. She made a cake."

"Hmm," Maratse said. He started to climb the steps, slowly, gritting his teeth and lifting each leg, and planting the sole of the heavy fishing boots on each step, before repeating the process. He had reached halfway when the girl's mother opened the door of their house and waved.

"Did Nanna invite you for cake?" she asked.

"*Iiji*," Maratse said.

"Will you come?"

"I need a shower," he said.

"Okay, maybe after your shower? It's good cake," she said, and smiled. Maratse noticed flour on her cheeks and trousers. She brushed at it when he nodded. "Great. I'll make fresh coffee."

Maratse waved and continued up the steps. The puppy worried at the heels of his boots as Maratse leaned against the railings to pull them off, tossing them halfway along the deck to distract the puppy as he opened the door and walked into his house. Maratse looked up at the stairs leading to the first floor and the bathroom, frowning at the flimsy banister. He unzipped the overalls and shrugged his way out of them, stealing himself for the climb only to stop when the phone rang. Maratse lifted his legs out of the overalls and hobbled into the living room. He picked up the telephone and leaned on the window sill.

"Piitalaat," he said.

"You knew it was me."

"You're the only one who has my number." Maratse thought for a moment. "I don't even know it." He smiled when he heard Petra laugh.

"I'm calling because of work."

"*Iiji.*"

"I'm just about to talk to Aarni Aviki."

"Who's he?"

"He's Uutaaq's communications chief. We think he can confirm that Malik was with Tinka just before she went missing."

"Piitalaat."

"Yes?"

"Why are you telling me?"

"Because…" Petra was quiet for a moment, and Maratse imagined her asking herself the same question. He heard her sigh, and then she said, "I trust you, and I need someone to talk to."

"Are you all right?"

"Yes," she said, and paused. "But the press is going to go nuts when they hear about the dead girl, especially if it is Tinka Winther's body that you fished out of the sea."

"It is," Maratse said.

"You're positive?"

"*Iiji.*"

Petra was quiet for a long time. Maratse waited. He glanced at the puppy chewing at the collar of one of Karl's boots on the deck. Maratse knocked on the window and growled. The puppy looked up, smoothing the expression on its face into one of pure innocence, with wide eyes, and a slight tilt of its head. Maratse growled again, and the puppy picked itself up and loped to the other end of the deck.

"David?" Petra said. "Did you just growl?"

"I have a puppy."

"That was fast."

"It wasn't my decision," he said, frowning as he realised he would have to feed it soon.

"But you're settling in. I mean, you're fishing and…"

"You're going to be okay, Piitalaat," Maratse said.

"I know but, I miss not having you here."

"We'll talk soon." Maratse waited for Petra to say goodbye and then placed the telephone on the cradle. It was an old model he realised. "Like I feel," he grunted, and looked towards the stairs, contemplating how old he would feel as he climbed them. He lifted the collar of his shirt, took a sniff, and decided he had to try.

Images of Tinka's body nagged at Maratse, as he climbed the stairs. He chewed over the details, pleased to have something to occupy his thoughts as he climbed, and again as he fiddled with an unfamiliar shower, and dried himself on the hand towel. Buuti's spare bath towels were still on the coffee table in the living room.

It was Tinka's clothes that bothered Maratse

most. The fact that she was wearing winter clothes, and yet, according to Petra, she had only been missing for a few days. The name tag was another curious detail, one that Maratse chose to think about as he climbed down the stairs, naked but for the hand towel around his neck. He rested against the wall in the hall, before walking into the living room and collapsing on the sofa. He pulled on his sweaty shirt and jogging trousers, and made a mental note to visit the store the next morning to buy what they had of clothes. The thought of fresh coffee encouraged Maratse to forget about Tinka for a while, and to get to know his neighbours. He made his way to the door, pushed his bare feet into his boots, and left the house. He growled once at the puppy for good measure, allowing himself a little smile as it retreated to the far end of the deck.

It was just one step from the beach onto the neighbour's deck, a detail not wasted on Maratse. He knocked on the door, and smiled as the little girl opened it.

"Hello," he said, and walked in as she pushed the door wide, and leaned against it.

"Don't get in the way, Nanna," her mother called from the kitchen. The house was the same type as Maratse's, but, unlike his house, the windowsills were overflowing with wings, bones, shells, stones, and skulls. He stared at the collection as Nanna guided him to a seat at the table by the window. She began handing him different things, and explaining what they were, when and where they had found them, and what her mother and her friend were going to do with them.

"Mummy is an artist," she said, as she placed a

raven claw in Maratse's palm.

"Hmm," Maratse said, as he pushed the skin of his thumb against the claws.

"I'm afraid it's true." Nanna's mother placed a large cake on a plate on the table, before returning to the kitchen for the coffee, mugs, and plates. She told Nanna to get the milk from the fridge, and gave her a gentle bump on her bottom with her foot as she passed. "I think that's everything," she said, as she sat down. She smiled at Maratse, held out her hand, and said, "I'm Sisse. My partner, Klara, is tramping along the beach somewhere."

"Maratse."

Sisse frowned, and said, "Just *Maratse*?"

"David," he said.

"Are you a policeman, David?" Sisse watched, as Nanna put the milk on the table. She pulled out a chair and helped her daughter sit down. "That's what we heard."

"I was."

"And now?"

"Retired," he said, and nodded when Sisse started to pour the coffee.

"What made you choose to move to Inussuk? Family?"

"Convenience. A nurse told me the house was available."

"A nurse? Have you been in hospital?"

"*Iiji.*" Maratse put the raven claw back on the windowsill.

"Is that East Greenlandic?" Sisse asked, and tried to repeat what Maratse had said.

"It means *yes* on the east coast."

"How interesting." Sisse helped Nanna pour milk

into her mug and smoothed her hand through her daughter's hair. "It seems that every time we hear the news – in Danish – it is about language, and how you can never truly be a Greenlander if you don't speak the language. What do you think about that, David?"

Maratse sipped at his coffee, as Sisse cut three slices of cake. He thought about Petra, and how the current debate was chipping away at her identity. A good officer, a good person, a good *Greenlander*, forced to consider her place in her own culture and country, for every day of the campaign until the elections, and maybe for the rest of her life. Sisse lifted a slice of cake onto a small plate and pushed it across the table to Maratse. She offered him a teaspoon, and then tried to catch his eye, in anticipation of his response.

"I don't like politics," he said.

"But it's all they talk about at the moment; on the radio, and the television. You can't escape it."

Maratse shrugged. "I don't listen to the radio. I don't have a television."

"What do you do for entertainment?"

Maratse cut a piece of cake, thumbing it onto the teaspoon when it slipped off. He nodded at the window and used the tip of the spoon to point at the icebergs, the mountains, and the sea. "And when it is dark," he said, and popped the cake into his mouth, "I read."

Nanna spilt some milk and made a fuss of getting a cloth from the kitchen to clean it up. Maratse ate his cake, pleased at the distraction, and content to look out of the window. Sisse helped her daughter to wipe the milk from the table, and Maratse sipped at his coffee, searching for a little patch of quiet in the storm of words that Danes seemed to need when eating a meal in company. But even when Nanna dragged her mother into the kitchen to clean the cloth, Maratse wasn't alone at the table, as images of Tinka occupied his thoughts, and he wondered if that part of his brain, the part that would always remain a policeman, would ever find peace, even in a place as small and secluded as Inussuk.

Chapter 12

Petra slipped her phone into her pocket and walked into the meeting room. She closed the door and offered Aarni Aviki a hot drink. When he declined, she poured a cup of coffee from the thermos and sat down at the table. She glanced at his hands as she arranged her notebook and a small digital Dictaphone that she placed between them. The communications chief for *Seqinnersoq* began to pick at his thumbnail. Petra watched, sipped her coffee, and waited. It was Aarni who spoke first, in Greenlandic.

"I want an interpreter," he said.

Petra turned on the Dictaphone, and said, "Can you repeat that, in Danish?"

"I asked for an interpreter."

"But your Danish is perfect, Mr Aviki."

"I have the right to an interpreter."

Petra pushed her coffee to one side and made a note on her pad. "I'm surprised you haven't asked for a lawyer," she said, and looked up. "Perhaps that would be more appropriate?"

Aarni stopped picking at his nail and sneered. "You're one of them," he said, switching to Danish, "the Danish-speaking Greenlanders."

Petra gripped the pen between her fingers and took a breath. "Lots of Greenlanders speak Danish, Mr Aviki."

"Yes, but they are from mixed parents. What's your excuse?"

"I didn't think I needed one," Petra said. She paused for a moment to take a breath. If she wasn't careful, she realised, this man could easily take her off-topic.

"I heard you grew up in the children's home, here in Nuuk," he said.

"Mr Aviki," Petra said, tapping her pencil on the table, "I would like to ask you some questions about your relationship to Tinka Winther."

"Your parents spoke Greenlandic," Aarni said, and leaned back in his chair. "Why don't you?"

Petra leaned over the Dictaphone and said, "Let the record show that Mr Aviki is evading the question." Petra paused to catch Aarni's eye. "And obstructing the investigation."

"Wait," Aarni said, "I'm not obstructing anything."

"Then answer the question, if you will. What is your relationship to Tinka Winther?"

"I don't have one. We have never met."

"But you know who she is?"

"After last night's news on television, doesn't everyone?"

"I'd like to hear you say it."

"Yes, I know who she is."

Petra made a note, scrawling a quick question beneath it. She reached for her coffee, took a sip, and then placed it on the table. "And Malik Uutaaq, do you know him?"

"Of course I do. He is the leader of my party, my boss." Aarni laughed. "That's a ridiculous question, Sergeant."

Petra ignored him, and made another note. She drew a line between the two. "What is Mr Uutaaq's relationship to Tinka Winther?"

Aarni glanced at the Dictaphone, and then at Petra's notes, squinting for a moment, as if he was trying to read them. He drummed his fingers on the table and looked around the room. He nodded at the thermos flask of coffee and Petra waited as he pushed back his chair and left the table. She noticed sweat on his brow when he returned. The surface of the coffee vibrated ever so slightly as he held the plastic cup in his hand. Petra repeated the question, as Aarni took a sip of coffee.

"Is this on record?" he asked, and glanced at the Dictaphone.

"I'm not a journalist," Petra said. "Everything is on record. Of course," she said, and pushed the notepad in front of Aarni, "if you wanted to write a statement instead…"

"No," he said, and put the cup down on the table.

Petra studied the man's eyes, and if she could see what Aarni was seeing, as he weighed his career against his political allegiance, she might have had some pity for the man's turmoil, as he considered his next move. As it was, she found only contempt for the man who had forced her to consider her own identity, and her place in the country of her birth. She enjoyed seeing him squirm, but still, his answer surprised her.

"No," he said. "Malik has no relationship with Tinka Winther, at least not that I am aware of."

"They have never met?"

"No."

"Perhaps in passing, at a party, for example?"

"Sergeant," Aarni said, and Petra could feel a renewed confidence in the man's demeanour, as if he had gained strength and a sense of peace with his decision to remain loyal to his boss, "I think we both know that Malik Uutaaq has a reputation for enjoying a good party. And why shouldn't he? What he does in his own time, is his own business."

"But when a girl goes missing, and his name is linked to her disappearance…"

"By whom, Sergeant? Who has linked Malik Uutaaq with the girl's disappearance?"

"That's not important. I am just following a lead."

"A lead?" Aarni stared at Petra. "And how many *leads* do you have?" Petra reached for the notepad and began to pull it across the table towards her. Aarni stopped her when he pressed his hand on the top page. "How many, Sergeant?"

"The way this works, Mr Aviki, is that I ask the questions, not you."

"And yet, you are suggesting my boss is involved in the disappearance of the daughter of his political opponent." Aarni let go of the notepad. "I am the communications chief for *Seqinnersoq*, and questions such as these, ones that have a direct influence on the party, are my domain. So, I ask you again, Sergeant, what leads do you have? How many are you pursuing?"

The sweat on Aarni's brow had evaporated. It seemed that the media onslaught since the beginning of the campaign had toughened Aarni Aviki's skin. Any sign of his earlier discomfort had disappeared, and Petra decided she needed to take a new tack, if she was going to get any useful information out of him. A shadow at the window, and a knock at the door caught them both by surprise, as did the identity of the person to enter the room.

"Ms Winther," Petra said, and stood up as Greenland's First Minister entered the room. "I'm sorry, but this is a private interview, and I am going to have to ask you to leave." She looked at Nivi's assistant as he appeared in the doorway.

Daniel Tukku nodded. "I'll handle this. Nivi?" he said. "We have to go. Your flight leaves in forty minutes."

Nivi ignored him and took a step closer to Aarni. She shook as she spoke, her lips trembling. "I have to fly to Uummannaq, to identify the body of a girl that could be my daughter. I heard that you know something," she said and glanced at Petra, "that you have information that might help the police find who did this to my daughter…"

"Nivi," Daniel said, as he placed a hand on her shoulder. He pulled her slowly away from the table, and towards the door.

"If you know anything," Nivi said, "you have to tell them. Because if you hide something, anything…" Nivi's voice grew stronger, as she straightened her back and took a breath. "I will make sure you are finished in Greenland, and I will expose you to the world."

"We have to go," Daniel said. He glanced at Aarni, and Petra caught the briefest of nods as Daniel guided Nivi out of the meeting room and along the office floor to the stairs. Petra closed the door. When she returned to the table, she picked up the Dictaphone, and turned it off. Aarni pointed at it.

"You have it on tape. She threatened me."

"She is upset."

"She was out of line. I could end her career with that tape."

"Police property," Petra said, and slipped the Dictaphone into her pocket. She looked at Aarni. "If you have nothing more to add, then you are free to go." She gestured at the door. "I think you know the way out."

Aarni pushed back his chair, and stood up. He finished his coffee, straightened his jacket and tie, and walked to the door.

"Just one thing," Petra said, as he closed his fingers around the door handle, "off the record."

Aarni looked at her, and said, "I thought everything was on the record, Sergeant."

"You're right, but this is personal."

"Go on."

"You think you're better than me, because you speak Greenlandic and I don't, but you're forgetting something, *Arne*." Petra waited for a second, as he registered her use of his Danish name. "Your mother is Danish. Your skin is lighter than mine. You had an excuse for not speaking Greenlandic in school. I didn't. And every time I tried, they told me that if I couldn't speak proper Greenlandic, then I shouldn't bother. And then they would hit me."

"Are you looking for sympathy, Sergeant?"

"No, not for me, but for the children, the coming generation. You're older than me. You were born after the first school reform, when Danish was prioritised."

The muscles in Aarni's face tightened. He glared at Petra. "That reform cursed me, and has cursed me my whole life. Me and my generation."

"That's right, it did," Petra said. "Just like you and your language extremism is cursing a whole new generation of Greenlanders. It cursed Tinka Winther, and now she is missing, and likely dead."

"You don't know that."

"That she is dead, or cursed? Does it matter?" Petra shrugged. "I know she couldn't speak Greenlandic. Her mother made no secret of that in the press."

"I don't know what you want to achieve with this little off-the-record chat, Sergeant, but I think we are done for the day." Aarni took his smartphone from his pocket and stepped out of the meeting room. Petra followed him.

"I have no more questions for you today, but you would be mistaken to think we are done. If the First Minister makes a positive identification of her daughter in Uummannaq, then this investigation changes gear again. If we discover that you withheld information, and this becomes an investigation of a suspicious death, perhaps even a murder, well…" Petra shrugged as Aarni stared at her. "Your reluctance to help and your lack of cooperation might just put you at the top of the list of people we would want to question, again, under less comfortable circumstances."

Aarni glanced at the screen of his phone, and slipped it back inside his pocket, wiping his hand on his trousers afterwards. Petra tapped the end of the pen against her chin.

"Have you just remembered something, Mr Aviki?"

"No," he whispered, and again, louder, "nothing."

"If you're sure?"

"Yes, I'm sure." Aarni looked around the office, and then glanced out of the window at the parking area. "I don't have a car," he said.

"I'm sure you'll manage."

Petra watched Aarni Aviki all the way to the door. As soon as he was gone, she walked across to the window, leaned against the wall beside her colleague's desk, and tilted her head for a better view of the main entrance below.

"That, Sergeant, might be considered stalking," the policeman said, and continued typing his report on the computer.

"It might."

"You wouldn't want that to come back and haunt you," he said, and laughed.

"Hush," she said. "I am looking out of the window. That's hardly stalking."

"He is Malik Uutaaq's spin doctor. If he sees you, he can choose to call it what he wants." Petra slapped her colleague on his shoulder with the notepad. He laughed again. "You just upgraded to abuse."

Petra ignored him as she watched Aarni. The glow from the screen of his smartphone lit his face as he began to punch in what she presumed was the number of a taxi service. He never made the call. A flash of headlights from a car parked opposite the main entrance caught Aarni's attention, and he put the phone back in his pocket. Petra watched him walk to the car and peer in through the driver's window. She couldn't see the driver, and the shadow cast by the police minibus parked nearby made it difficult to see if it was a man or a woman sitting in the driver's seat. Aarni stepped back and waited for the car to pull out before getting into the passenger seat. Petra switched her attention to the number plate, but it was obscured with dirt. She reached out and grabbed her colleague by the shoulder.

"Quick," she said, "see if you can read the

number of that car."

The police officer pushed back his chair and stood up, pressing his face to the window as the car below them pulled out of the car park and into the street.

"Sorry," he said. "I didn't see it."

"A black Suzuki," Petra said, and made a note on her pad.

"Do you think it's important?"

"Who knows, but right now, it's all in the details."

She walked back to her desk and sat down on the office chair, dropping her pad beside the computer keyboard as she moved backwards and forwards in the chair, tapping her chin with the end of the pen. Whoever was in the car was waiting for Aarni, but Petra couldn't recall him calling anyone, or sending a text message during her brief interview. Gaba had him too spooked to call anyone on the ride to the station. Petra smiled at the thought – Gaba had that effect on people. No, she decided, whoever was waiting for Aarni had discovered he was at the police station without him contacting anyone. Petra just didn't know if it was important.

"Another small detail," she whispered to herself.

Petra wheeled the chair to the desk and moved the computer mouse to refresh the screen. She typed in her password and checked her intranet messages. There was nothing new. She typed up her notes and thought about what the First Minister had said about flying to Uummannaq. A positive identification would take the case in a new direction, and create a potential frenzy in the media, both in Greenland, and likely in Denmark too.

Petra finished with her notes and leaned back in the chair. She checked her watch, and then looked at the clock on the wall. She had ten minutes before her shift ended. The convenient arrival of someone to give Aarni Aviki a lift from the station intrigued her, but it was something that could wait until tomorrow.

Tallimanngorneq

FRIDAY

Chapter 13

Maratse watched the hotel boat moor at the jetty. There was a small buzz of people waiting for Nivi Winther and her ex-husband to arrive, Karl and his wife, Buuti, among them. The news of Nivi's positive identification of her daughter's body had spread quickly, and the preparations for her funeral had been arranged shortly afterwards.

Maratse sipped at his coffee as Karl and Edvard helped Martin Winther, and three other men, lift the coffin containing Tinka Winther from the deck, and carry it along the jetty to the beach. Nivi walked behind the men carrying her daughter to the graveyard overlooking the fjord and the people of Inussuk followed. There were at least three reporters among the mourners, and it surprised Maratse that Nivi seemed not to notice when they took her picture at various points along the way. But then, her level of grief was probably such that she didn't care, certainly not before the pictures were on the front pages of the newspapers, at which time it would already be too late. Maratse finished his coffee and straightened the black tie he had borrowed from Karl.

He walked to the hall, pleased that he had learned to ignore the pain in his legs. He slipped his feet inside his boots. It was still a trial to tie his own laces, but the stairs were useful. When he was finished with his boots, he heaved himself onto his feet with one hand on the banister and the other on the windowsill. When he walked out onto the deck the puppy looked up from where it guarded the seal bone Maratse had given it, something to occupy it while he was away.

"Is that the First Minister?" Sisse asked, from

where she stood on the deck of her house.

"*Iiji*," Maratse said, and walked down the steps to the beach.

"Do you think I can go up there?" Sisse pointed at the procession of family and mourners following the men carrying Tinka Winther up the steep side of the mountain. "Or would it be inappropriate?"

"I'm going," Maratse said. "You can come with me."

Sisse reached inside the door of her house and grabbed her jacket. Her partner offered to keep an eye on Nanna while she was away. She pulled on her jacket and jogged to catch up with Maratse, as he walked along the beach towards the path. The sky was heavy with snow, and the first flakes fell as Sisse tugged the zip all the way to the collar. She stuffed her hands in her pockets and switched sides to avoid the smoke from Maratse's cigarette. They climbed in silence, stopping several times as Maratse took a break. When they reached the graveyard the service was nearly over, and the snow fell heavily on the mourners.

"Let's wait here." Maratse stood to one side of the white picket fence that ran around three sides of the graveyard. The cliff face served as the fourth and final side, a natural barrier protecting the dead from the sea. Maratse stuffed the stub of his cigarette inside the packet and tucked it into his jacket pocket. He blinked in the flash of a reporter's camera, and realised that he probably should have borrowed an overcoat from his neighbour too. The yellow and green police emblem on his jacket was clearly visible on the right breast.

"They are taking our picture," Sisse said, as the

two other reporters joined the first in documenting what the papers would probably report as a police presence at the funeral.

"Hmm," Maratse said. He ignored the cameras and watched as Nivi laid a wreath of plastic flowers beside her daughter's grave. Karl and Edvard would arrange the flowers on top of the grave later, but for now, as the snow fell, so did the flowers, as the mourners took turns to place a wreath before saying their last goodbyes and walking down the mountain for the wake. Buuti had arranged it, and agreed with the present occupants of Nivi Winther's childhood home, that they would hold it there. It was to be a small gathering, she had explained to Maratse.

Maratse watched as Nivi put her arm around Tinka's father, pulling him close as he sagged at the side of the grave. He slipped to his knees. Nivi laid one hand on his shoulder and clasped the other over her mouth. Her sobs were quiet, but they filtered through the snowfall blanketing the graveyard.

"Why are they leaving plastic flowers?" Sisse whispered.

"Have you seen real flowers in Greenland?"

"No," she said. "But plastic..."

"Is forever," he said, and watched as Nivi pulled away from her ex-husband, and searched for a way out between the mourners, somewhere she could be alone, just for a moment. She started to walk away from the grave, saw Maratse, and walked straight towards him, growing stronger with each step. She smiled at Sisse as she approached and then looked at Maratse.

"You're a policeman?" she asked.

"I was," he said. "My name is Maratse." He

shook her hand, surprised at how cool and firm it was.

"You found my daughter."

"*Iiji*," he said, and nodded at Karl standing close to the grave. "We found her."

"Thank you," she said. "It must have been difficult." Nivi looked at Sisse, and said, "Please excuse us." She hooked her arm through Maratse's and walked with him towards the edge of the mountain, pausing as he slowed. "You're hurt?"

"It's nothing," he said. "I'm recovering from an injury."

Nivi nodded and let go of his arm. Snow brushed her short hair as she looked out at the fjord, glancing once at the mourners as they passed and began to walk down the path. "I grew up here. Perhaps you knew that?"

"*Iiji*," Maratse said. He turned as Martin Winther was guided down the path, and Karl and Edvard began to cover Tinka's coffin. They were alone but for the soft slice of the spades in the dirt.

"Tinka and I used to come up here, when her grandparents were still alive. We climbed this path every day," she said, and pointed to a small knoll to one side. "We would sit there and watch for whales." Nivi caught a tear as it rolled down her cheek and wiped it away. "That's why I wanted to bury her here, so that she can look for whales. Is that silly?"

"*Eeqqi*," Maratse said. "It is a good place."

"You're from the east? Tasiilaq?"

"Ittoqqortoormiit."

"But you chose to move here?"

"For a while."

"Why?"

"A new start."

"I understand," she said. "I need your help, Constable." Nivi looked at Maratse. She took a breath and bit her bottom lip, as if she was making a decision, wondering if it was the right one.

"I'm not a policeman anymore," he said.

"But you still wear the jacket?"

Maratse shrugged. "It is a good jacket."

Nivi tried to smile, and said, "I want you to find out how my daughter died. I know," she said, as Maratse started to speak, "Sergeant Jensen is working on the case, and the Commissioner himself has assured me they are doing everything they can, but…" Nivi sighed and clenched her fists. She looked out to the sea, licked a stray tear from her lip, and took a deep breath. "I just don't think they have the necessary drive to find the answers."

"Drive? I don't understand."

Nivi tried another smile. "Forgive me, what I meant to say was I'm not sure they are stubborn enough."

"And you think I am?" Maratse frowned.

"Stubborn enough to walk up a mountain when you are clearly in pain," she said with a glance at Maratse's legs.

"I don't know," he said. "I have friends in the Nuuk police department. Sergeant Jensen, for example."

"And I have the greatest respect for Sergeant Jensen, but she will be tied by time and the law."

"I will not do anything against the law," Maratse said.

"Gosh, no, I don't mean that you should. But you could ask questions, in an unofficial capacity.

Anything you learn, you could pass on to the police, to Sergeant Jensen."

Maratse shifted on his feet, biting back a flash of pain. "I don't think it is a good idea," he said. "I'm not the right person to help you."

"I think, Constable, that you are exactly that person, and I also think that it is no accident that you are here, in Inussuk, and that it was you who found my daughter."

"I don't know." Maratse shook his head. "I think…"

"Please," Nivi said, and reached out to touch his arm. She pulled back her hand and took a breath. "They examined Tinka in the hospital. The official report says that she died in a boating accident. But what was she doing in a boat, here of all places? I need help, Constable," she said. "Don't decide now. I am leaving tomorrow. We can talk in the morning. I will also pay you," she said, and added, "from my own pocket. Unlike some of my colleagues, I do not believe in dipping into the party war chest when it becomes convenient." She pressed her lips into a tight smile. "If you can help me help the police, and find out how my daughter died, then you will give me the peace of mind I need to move on." She tilted her head and looked Maratse in the eye. "Can you do that?"

"I will think about it," he said.

"Thank you." Nivi squeezed his arm and looked over at Tinka's grave, as Karl and Edvard laid the flowers over the soil and snow. "I heard they buried a baby last Monday, and now they have buried mine. Perhaps they will give each other some comfort." The snow crunched beneath Nivi's boots as she walked towards the path and made her way down the mountainside.

Maratse watched her leave, and cursed himself for being so fond of his jacket. And yet, he wore it for a reason. He wasn't ready to let go of his former life, not just yet. Perhaps he should help Nivi Winther discover what happened to her daughter? Had he not already speculated about the clothes Tinka was wearing when he pulled her out of the water? The name tag intrigued him. But Petra was working the case, and he knew she would keep him informed, no matter how much he pretended not to be interested.

He tapped a cigarette into his hand from the packet in his pocket, lit it and rolled it into the gap between his teeth. He waved at Karl and walked to the graveyard, stopping every other step to draw a cloud of smoke into his lungs, and to allow the pain to settle in his legs. When he reached the grave he offered Karl and Edvard a smoke, lighting their cigarettes before slipping the lighter inside the packet. It had been a small private funeral, and would remain so until the reporters returned to their hotel rooms in Uummannaq and uploaded the images. He could hear the engines of the hotel boat cough and start as they smoked, and soon he would be able to see it, as it sped across the fjord to the town.

"Five," Karl said, as he finished his cigarette.

"What's that?"

"Five graves left." He bent down to extinguish the cigarette butt in the snow, and then slipped it into his jacket pocket. He nodded at the remaining graves.

"And if it is not enough?" Maratse asked. "What then?"

"That depends on the winter," Edvard said and

glanced up at the sky.

"Hmm," Maratse said.

Karl and Edvard picked up their shovels and started walking towards the path. They waited for Maratse, but he waved them on, pointing at his legs.

"I'll be there later," he said. He watched them leave until they disappeared from view, and then he looked down at Tinka's grave. "Your mother wants me to find out what happened to you. What do *you* want?"

Maratse lit another cigarette, taking his time to light it, as if the longer he took, the more time Tinka would have to think it over. The truth was, he knew, that the decision was his, and the dead were dead, forever. He smoked as the skies darkened from graphite to charcoal, and the first real night of winter descended on Inussuk. He realised the path would be obscured, and also that he didn't care.

"I'd have to travel," he said, his voice loud in the cocoon of snow swirling around the graveyard. "And what would Petra think?" He smiled at the thought of seeing her again, and at the realisation that he was speaking more to himself and to a dead girl, than he usually did in the company of others.

He turned at the sound of something padding across the snow. The puppy slowed as it approached the entrance to the graveyard, and Maratse growled a command to stop it before it passed through the gate. Maratse walked away from Tinka's grave, but carried her with him in his thoughts as he followed the puppy down the mountainside, past the store, all the way to Nivi's family home. The lights were on and there were candles burning in the windows. Nivi was alone on the deck as he climbed the steps, one at a time, and turned to shoo the puppy back to the beach.

"Is it yours?" Nivi asked as he joined her on the deck.

"I think it is."

"Soul mates," she said and pointed at the puppy. It rested on the snow, eyes fixed on Maratse. "Have you thought about what I asked you?"

"You said I had until tomorrow."

"I did," Nivi said, "but I think you have made your decision already."

"*Iiji*," he said.

"And?"

"If I help you, I will share everything I find with Sergeant Jensen, before I tell you."

Nivi nodded. "If that's important to you."

"It is."

"Then I accept," she said.

Maratse thought for a second, and then said, "I don't know what to call myself."

"Call yourself?" The candlelight flickered across the wrinkles on Nivi's brow. "I don't understand?"

"I'm not a policeman anymore. Private investigator fits, but I don't like the sound of it," he said, and shrugged, chewing over the title in his mind.

"How about my own private Constable, if that makes you feel easier?"

Maratse nodded. "I suppose it doesn't matter."

"Everything matters, Constable," Nivi said. "Everything *should* matter. Just like my daughter's death should matter." Nivi brushed the snow from the shoulders of her jacket. "Come on, there is food inside, and it's cold out here." She tucked her arm through Maratse's and walked with him to the door.

Maratse heard the telephone ring as he climbed

the steps to his house after the wake. He grunted as he kicked off his shoes and walked to the window to pick up the phone.

"Maratse," he said, as he held the receiver to his ear.

"This is Simonsen."

"Hmm."

"Have you forgotten what we talked about on the boat?"

"*Eeqqi.*"

"I don't speak Greenlandic," Simonsen said.

"No, I haven't forgotten."

"Then why did I just get a call from someone telling me about you helping the First Minister? Investigating her daughter's death? Do I have to remind…?"

Maratse ended the call and made his way to the sofa. He slumped onto the cushions, reached for his book on the coffee table, and started to read. Simonsen's veiled threats were forgotten as he concentrated on the small English type in the thick book, distracted in part by the thought of travelling back to Nuuk with the First Minister the following day. He caught a smile as it twitched at the corners of his lips, leaned back and closed his eyes.

Arfininngorneq

SATURDAY

Chapter 14

Petra locked the door of the police Toyota and splashed through the slush to the airport entrance. She held her breath as she passed through the clouds of cigarette smoke from the passengers who were taking a break between flights, or waiting for taxis. Once through the waiting lounge she knocked on the door to the tiny baggage reclaim and arrivals area. The police officer on duty glanced at her through the glass and let her in.

"Here to pick someone up?" she asked.

"Yes. How about you, Atii? Busy?"

Atii Napa grinned and gestured at the empty arrivals area. "What do you think?" She waited for Petra to enter the room, and locked the door behind her. "Actually," she said, "we have a person of interest arriving from Kangerlussuaq later today. I think you know him."

"Who?"

"Mala Toori." Atii raised her eyebrows and waited for Petra to remember the name.

"It's a while since I last heard his name," she said, remembering when she and Maratse searched for a missing girl in a container.

"*Aap*," Atii said. "He has been quiet for a long time, but we had a tip that he may be back in the business of smuggling hash. Not personally, but coordinating it. The narco cops want a word with him."

"And that's why you're here?"

"No, I got dumped with customs duty when Søren called in sick this morning. But picking up Mala makes life a little more interesting. How about you?"

"I'm here to meet David Maratse."

"I heard something about him. He had an accident, and got early retirement."

"Yep, but I have a feeling he is finding it hard to retire." She recalled the message she had received from the Commissioner, something about Nivi Winther hiring Maratse as a private investigator. If it was true, it would make Maratse the first private investigator she knew of in Greenland. Petra's lips twitched at the thought, but her smile faded when she remembered that the Commissioner was less than pleased about Maratse's new role. Regardless, Petra was excited to see him, and she walked to the window at the sound of the Dash 8 from Ilulissat taxiing to the apron outside arrivals.

"Now you're here," Atii said, reaching out to touch Petra's arm as the ground crew directed the aircraft to a stop.

"Yes?"

"Are you still seeing Gaba?"

"No," Petra said. She looked Atii in the eye. "You don't have to ask permission. It's not like I own him."

"I know. It's just a bit weird, you know?"

"I know." Petra shrugged, as Atii walked over to the arrivals door to receive the passengers. "Good luck," she said, as Atii waved.

Petra's first surprise was seeing Maratse walk towards her without the use of sticks, and the second was his pace as he walked, side-by-side with Nivi Winther. Petra studied the First Minister for signs of grief, she had expected her to be distraught, but it seemed that the tragic conclusion to her daughter's disappearance had boosted her resolve. She looked every inch the right person to lead the country, regardless of what the polls might say. The popular vote still favoured Malik Uutaaq, and Petra didn't know how Nivi Winther was going to change that. It wasn't long before she had her first taste of the minister's new direction and sense of purpose.

"Sergeant Jensen," Nivi said, as she entered arrivals, "you remember Constable Maratse?"

"I do," Petra said, and smiled at Maratse. "Although, I remember him retiring, too."

"He's my Constable now, Sergeant."

Maratse shifted from one foot to the other as the women talked about him. Petra noticed he had removed the police emblem from his jacket, but he still looked every inch a policeman. The thought gave her a warm feeling. Nivi explained the arrangement that had been agreed, that Maratse would be keeping Petra informed of his progress.

The doors to the waiting lounge opened again as Daniel Tukku walked through. Petra caught the look that Daniel shot at Maratse, before he greeted the First Minister and took her bag.

"This is a little weird," Petra said, as she walked with Maratse to the car. "And you seem better. No sticks."

"It still hurts," he said, and got into the passenger side as Petra unlocked it.

Petra climbed in behind the wheel and closed the door. She waited for a second. "The Commissioner wanted me to pick you up. But it's a bit more complicated than that."

"He doesn't want me to get in the way."

"He's worried you might. And we don't know why you are here."

"Nivi wants me to find out how her daughter died."

"But we are doing that."

"I know," Maratse said, and looked at Petra, "but that's why I'm here."

"I'm pleased," Petra said, smiling as she started the engine.

Petra drove out of the parking area and into town, glancing at Maratse, as he looked out of the window. The sun crowned the summit of Sermitsiaq with a golden glow, in stark contrast to the grey slush that stuck to the wheels of the cars on the streets of Nuuk.

Maratse sighed. "Where are you taking me, Piitalaat?"

"Where do you want to go?"

"Nivi said I should talk to Aarni Aviki."

"I interviewed him yesterday," Petra said. She wrinkled her nose at the thought. "It didn't go well, and he didn't say much."

"Perhaps he will say more to me?"

"Because you're a man?"

"Because I'm not the police," Maratse said, and shrugged. "I can try. This is all new to me."

"It's new to Greenland." Petra slowed at a roundabout. "But he seems to have gone into hiding overnight. I have been calling him all morning. Maybe you should talk to Qitu Kalia, the journalist?"

"Why?"

"I think he knows something, but we have no reason to interview him. Perhaps you could, unofficially?"

"I could. And there is Malik Uutaaq."

"No," Petra said. She curled a loose strand of hair

around her ear as she drove. "I would stay away from him today."

"Why?"

"The clothes you found on Tinka Winther. You told me they had the name Uutaaq in them. We are going to pick him up after the debate on Sunday."

"Why not today?"

"The Commissioner doesn't want our actions to look politically motivated. If we pick him up today, people might think we are trying to influence the outcome." She looked at Maratse. "A lot of people will be watching. It could decide the election."

"Hmm," Maratse said. He leaned back against the headrest.

Petra laughed. "For someone who doesn't like politics or politicians, you are in the middle of it now."

"I know."

Maratse put his hand in his pocket and pulled out a mobile phone. "Nivi said I had to have one. I should give you the number."

Petra slowed, and then pulled off the road to park outside the offices of the *Sermitsiaq* newspaper. She turned off the engine and pulled on the handbrake, pushing the errant strand of hair behind her ear again as she lifted her head to look at Maratse.

"What's the number?"

"I don't know," he said, and handed her the mobile.

Petra unlocked the mobile and clicked a few buttons before taking out her smartphone and adding Maratse's mobile to her contact list. "I'm adding my number to your contacts, too," she said, returning his mobile to him when she was finished.

"*Qujanaq,*" he said, and leaned forwards to peer up at the sign on the building. The outline of Nuuk's most famous mountain rested above its name and the name of the media company. "Qitu Kalia works here?"

"Yes." Petra tapped the steering wheel. "I will wait as long as I can, but the Commissioner made it clear that we are not working the case together. As much as I might like to." Petra smiled.

Maratse opened the door, took a moment to prepare for the flash of pain he knew would come as soon as his feet touched the ground, and then got out of the car. He gritted his teeth and then looked at Petra. "It is good to see you, Piitalaat. Thank you for the ride."

"It's good to see you, too. Where are you staying?"

"Nivi has booked me a room at Hotel Hans Egede."

"Okay," Petra said. "I'll call you."

Petra's smartphone began to ring, and she waited for Maratse to shut the door before answering it. He heard her start the car and turn on the siren before he reached the door of the building. The blue flash of emergency lights flickered in his vision and was gone. Maratse paused, his hand on the door, as he thought about the last time he had driven at speed with the blue lights flashing, and the siren blaring. He pushed the image from his mind and opened the door.

The receptionist directed Maratse to the second floor. He grimaced at the thought, and then started to climb the stairs. Qitu Kalia met him in the corridor by the stairwell, shook his hand, and showed him to his office. Maratse decided that the journalist must be successful to have his own office, and was pleased to be offered a comfortable chair on the other side of Qitu's desk. Maratse started to speak in Greenlandic, only to stop when Qitu raised his hand.

"Danish, please. It is easier to lip read."

"You can't lip read in Greenlandic?"

"I can, but you are from the east coast?"

"*Iiji*," Maratse said.

"It is difficult to understand you."

"Danish then."

"Thank you," Qitu said. He stared at Maratse's lips. "How can I help you?"

"What can you tell me about Tinka Winther?"

"Are you still with the police?"

"No. I am working for Nivi."

"The First Minister?" Qitu made a note on the pad on his desk. "As a private investigator?" he asked, and looked up to study Maratse's lips.

Maratse nodded. "Is there a connection between Aarni Aviki and Tinka Winther?"

"Not that I know of," Qitu said. "What will you do with the answers I give you? Will you give them to Nivi, or the police?"

"Both," Maratse said. "Police first."

"Why should I tell you anything? If there was anything to tell?"

"Because a girl is dead."

Qitu made another note on his pad, and then stood up. "Coffee?" He left the office, returning a few minutes later with two mugs of coffee. He put them on the desk and shut the door. When he sat down, Maratse thought there was something different about the journalist. He thanked Qitu for the coffee and waited.

"I write about a lot of things," Qitu said, "but recently, it is mostly politics."

Maratse sipped at his coffee and wished for a cigarette.

"What do you think about the politics of *Seqinnersoq*? Do you agree with them?"

"I don't like politics," Maratse said.

"But you work for a politician."

Maratse shrugged, and took another sip of coffee. "I am interested in what happened to the girl," he said. "Her mother just happens to be a politician."

"I think you're wrong about that," Qitu said. "I think the two things are closely connected. This election…" He paused to stand up and move his chair closer to Maratse. "This election is corrupt, and I think the issue of language is being used as a diversion."

"You think Malik Uutaaq is hiding something?"

"Yes, but not what you think. I think other people are using the politics of *Seqinnersoq* to hide much more."

"Such as Tinka's death?"

"I don't know," Qitu said, and glanced at the window in the door as someone walked past his office. "In the beginning I was angry at the way Malik Uutaaq and Aarni Aviki used language as a weapon. I had access to Nivi Winther's campaign, and was encouraged to write a piece to expose Malik's double-standards, his hypocrisy, and his lust for young women of mixed blood." Qitu shrugged. "I thought it was the right thing to do, and that I could help change the narrative."

"But you didn't?" Maratse said. "Why?"

"I think I was just being used."

"By who?"

"Daniel Tukku."

"Nivi's assistant?"

"Yes. He is popular among the businesses in Nuuk, and he has a lot of contacts abroad. He has made a lot of promises, promises he can't keep if his party does not win the election."

"It's not his party," Maratse said.

"Not yet. But if Nivi was to stand down, if something happened to make her think about her future with the party. Perhaps something that made other people question if she was fit to lead. A family tragedy, for example. Something traumatic."

"Like the death of her daughter."

"Something like that, yes."

"She has not stepped down."

"Not yet."

Qitu let the thought hang in the air between them. He reached for his coffee, and leaned back in his chair. Maratse bit his lip and moved his legs, fidgeting for a more comfortable position. Qitu watched him.

"The receptionist said you were a policeman, but you have removed your badge, and now you are calling yourself a private investigator."

"You called me that," Maratse said.

"I did. But maybe it doesn't matter what you are called. Maybe you are being used, like me." Qitu finished his coffee and pointed at Maratse's legs. "I think you have been used before."

"Why?"

"Something I heard about you. Something no-one talks about. But there was a car chase here in Nuuk, just before the summer."

"It wasn't me."

"And a fire, at a mine. They said it was an accident."

"I don't know what you are talking about," Maratse said.

"I think you do, but I also think you are loyal," Qitu said. "I like that. I think you are a good Greenlander. You are good for this country."

"Hmm," Maratse said. "Maybe."

"Perhaps we can help each other."

"I thought we already were?"

"Yes, but if you let me write this story, I can help the people of Greenland to make the right choice for the future of Greenland."

"And what is that?"

"The truth. They must vote for the truth."

Maratse shifted position and put his mug on the desk. He stood up, took a moment to find his balance, and then held out his hand. "*Qujanaq*," he said, and shook Qitu's hand. "I think I have enough for now."

"Will you talk to Daniel Tukku?"

"I think I should."

"I think so too," Qitu said. "But please, talk to me again. We can help each other."

Maratse nodded, and walked towards the door. He stopped to answer his mobile, and smiled at the caller's name displayed on the screen.

"Piitalaat," he said.

"David," Petra said.

Something in her voice made Maratse frown. He held the mobile close to his ear and turned his back on the journalist. "What is it?"

Petra took a breath. "We've found Aarni Aviki. I

think you need to come and look."

Chapter 15

The taxi driver slowed the black Mercedes, as the policeman in the middle of the road waved for him to stop. The snow in the north had yet to turn into anything more than sleet in Nuuk, and the policeman was wet. As he tipped his cap the rain dribbled off the peak. Maratse paid the taxi driver, got out, and the Mercedes disappeared into the black evening, back the way it had come. Maratse waited a moment for the pain to subside in his legs, and then approached the policeman.

"I can't let you any closer," he said.

"Sergeant Jensen is expecting me," Maratse said. The policeman looked doubtful. Maratse pointed to the two police cars parked in front of a twenty foot container, the headlights of each car illuminated the interior. Maratse could see Petra, pinned between the beams of light, and he pointed at her. "She's just there. You could ask her."

The policeman looked over his shoulder, and nodded. "Wait here." The policeman cut the cone of blue flashing lights from the nearest police car with his body. Maratse studied the blue pearls of rain on the surface of the road, caught in the same flash of emergency, as he wondered what Petra wanted to show him. He started walking as soon as the policeman waved for him to come.

Petra was busy talking to a doctor and a paramedic as they examined the body of a man inside the container. She waved at Maratse to come forward, and then looked up at the body. A voice in Maratse's ear made him turn and he looked up at the face of Gaba Alatak, who was wearing plain clothes.

"Suicide," Gaba said.

"Aarni Aviki?"

"Yep." Gaba brushed his hand through his thick black hair, releasing a shower of water that caught the light. For a moment, Maratse was impressed by the sight of the SRU officer haloed in blue, before Gaba dropped his hand to his side. "I don't think you should be here, Maratse."

"I understand."

"Do you?" Gaba tugged at the sleeve of Maratse's jacket. "You're still in uniform."

"It's a good jacket," Maratse said. He offered Gaba a cigarette, but he declined. Maratse lit one for himself. "You're not in uniform. What are you doing here?"

"The Commissioner called me." Gaba wiped the rain from his face. "Apparently, the Chief of Police in Uummannaq has some concerns."

"Hmm." Maratse took a long drag on his cigarette.

"He thinks you are too involved in the case. He even suggested your involvement was suspicious. That there are too many unanswered questions about you and your past, not to make you a person of interest – someone we should keep an eye on."

"What did the Commissioner say?" Maratse caught a brief smile on Gaba's face.

"He said your past was your own, and that you were now retired from the force." Gaba looked at Maratse. "Of course, that's a little difficult to see."

"*Iiji.*"

"The Commissioner also said we were to cooperate with you. So, I can tell you Aarni left a note – a recording. We found a Dictaphone in his jacket pocket." He pointed at the door of the container. "People think you have to hang from something high in order to die, but it's not true. I've found people dead with a tie around their throat, lying on the floor next to their bed. If they had propped themselves up on an elbow they could have survived. Aviki's feet were on the ground, I mean, if he stretched his toes he could have held himself up…" Gaba paused. "Until he got tired, of course."

"You're not sure it was suicide?"

"That's what the doctors are trying to figure out. There's a chair inside. My guess is, if it's not suicide, then someone could have sat in the chair and watched him try to keep himself up, until he couldn't any longer."

"How long has he been dead?"

"Several hours. Of course, if this wasn't suicide, and you consider what he said on the tape, if someone was trying to get him to say something specific, it might have taken a while. There's an echo on the recording. It sounds like it was made inside the container. Out of sight." Gaba stared at Maratse through a cloud of cigarette smoke. "About your past – there's a rumour you were tortured."

"Hmm," Maratse said. He flicked at the filter of his cigarette with his tongue.

"But you don't talk about it?"

"*Eeqqi,*" he said, and shook his head.

Gaba sighed. "I can't imagine it. I would probably tell them anything they wanted to hear."

Maratse tossed his cigarette butt onto the road. "The man who tortured me didn't ask any questions. He didn't want a confession." He looked at Gaba, and waited for him to step to one side.

"Fair enough," Gaba said.

"Petra is waving at us," Maratse said, and gestured at the container. "Shall we go over there?"

"You go ahead, I have to get my team ready." Gaba started to walk away.

"For what?"

"To pick up Malik Uutaaq," he said, and raised his eyebrows. "Talk to Petra. She'll fill you in." He paused for a moment. "Don't worry about Simonsen. The Commissioner let slip that you might not be the only one to get early retirement." Gaba shrugged. "Just keep it legal, *Constable*."

Maratse watched Gaba walk to a black SUV parked behind the police Toyotas. He waited until Gaba had driven away before walking between the police cars and into the container. Petra stopped him just inside the door, out of the rain.

The smell of urine was heavy inside the container, and Maratse considered lighting another cigarette. He studied Aarni's inert body as the paramedic checked the chain around Aarni's neck. It was too thick to cut with regular bolt cutters, so Aarni would hang until the firefighters arrived to cut him down. He flinched when Petra touched his arm.

"Are you okay?"

"*Iiji*," Maratse said.

"Do you want to go outside?"

"It's raining. It's better here." Maratse nodded at Aviki. "Gaba said there was a note?"

"Yes," Petra said.

"He said it was interesting."

"And incriminating," she said.

At the sound of sirens blaring down the hill towards them, Petra tapped Maratse's arm and pointed at the nearest police car. They got in and closed the doors as the first fire engine arrived. Petra pulled a Dictaphone from her pocket.

"This is a recording of the message on the Dictaphone we found in Aviki's pocket. They rushed the original back to the station, to transcribe it." She pressed play, and Maratse stared at the recording device in her hands. Aarni Aviki's voice echoed just as Gaba had described it. Petra pressed a button to fast forward the tape, and then turned up the volume. Aarni's voice stuttered into the space between them.

...I already told the police. I never met Tinka Winther.

There was a click, as if the recording had been stopped, and then Aarni's voice continued.

Yes, he did meet with her.

Another click.

Malik Uutaaq.

"That's what I asked him at the station," Petra said, and stopped the recording. "We were told that Aviki can confirm that Malik Uutaaq knew Tinka Winther, and that he was probably the last person to be with her. Maybe the last person to see her alive."

Maratse glanced out of the window, as the fire crew carried a pair of hydraulic cutters from the fire engine into the container.

"Did Daniel Tukku tell you that?"

"What?"

"Was he the one who said Aviki could confirm Uutaaq was with Tinka?"

"Yes," Petra said, as a frown wrinkled her forehead. "Why?"

"The journalist thinks Tukku is trying to frame Uutaaq."

The shudder of a generator and the slow screech

of the hydraulic cutters biting through the thick links of chain prevented further conversation until the fire crew were finished, and Aarni Aviki was carried out of the container on a stretcher. The doctor knocked on the window of the police car, and Petra opened it.

"We're taking his body straight to the morgue. We'll do a thorough examination, and then contact you if there's any reason to think we need to do an autopsy. As it is, it looks like a straightforward suicide. But," he said with a nod at the Dictaphone in Petra's hand, "that makes it a little more interesting." The doctor turned at a shout from the paramedic and her driver. "Yes, go, I'll meet you there." He wiped the rain from his face and looked at Petra, as the siren of the ambulance cut through the air.

"You can call the station when you know more," she said, and pulled her smartphone from her pocket. The doctor slapped the door and jogged to his own car. He was already gone by the time Petra was finished with updating the duty officer at the station. She put her smartphone on the dashboard and leaned back in the seat, turned her head to one side and tried to smile at Maratse. "It's been a long day," she said. "Tell me again about Tukku."

"He's made a lot of promises to a lot of people, businesses, countries…"

"Countries?"

Maratse shrugged, and said, "That's what the journalist said."

"So, how does this fit with Tinka?"

"Tukku needs to be in power. He needs to be the one who can make decisions."

"And Malik Uutaaq is too popular, and too powerful," Petra said. She sighed. "I'm beginning to see why you hate politics." She turned as the policeman from the road knocked on the window.

"The fire chief is done. What now?"

"Seal the container for the night. We've documented what we can. The investigative team can continue in the morning."

"And then I can go on my break?"

"Yes," Petra said, cursing the young man as he tipped his cap and a pool of water cascaded onto the window of the police car, splashing Petra's cheeks. He grinned and jogged to the container to shut and padlock the doors.

"So," she said, and started the engine, "I'm cold, wet, and I need food. What about you?" Maratse nodded and Petra reversed into the road, and drove up the hill towards the centre of town. She parked outside a Thai restaurant a few minutes later, and they found an empty booth beyond the buffet tables. Petra ordered for both of them, and then put her notebook on the table. "The Commissioner will want to know what our next move is."

"Our next move?" The muscles in Maratse's face twitched as he stretched his legs into a more comfortable position. "You mean yours?"

"Yes, and *ours*, the two of us. We're working together. That's what Nivi Winther wants, and the Commissioner is playing along with her, for the moment at least. So," Petra said, and smiled, "we're partners."

"Partners." Maratse unzipped the front of his jacket and laughed for a moment. He realised he hadn't laughed for a while, and the fact that he was working again, police work, turned the laugh into a smile.

"You're happy," Petra said.

"I'm working."

The waitress brought two cardboard boxes of food and two large cokes. "In case we have to leave," Petra said when Maratse frowned at the box of noodles and sauce. She peeled back the four sides of the lid, and pushed the disposable chopsticks through the paper wrapping. Maratse picked up a fork.

"Why exactly was Gaba at the container?" he said, and opened the box of food.

"You heard the recording. The Commissioner promised the First Minister that Gaba would be involved in all aspects of the case. Aviki's suicide is a new development."

"If it really was suicide?"

"Yes, I mean if some guy forced Aviki to confess…"

"A man?"

"Maybe," Petra said, and pinched a king prawn between the chopsticks. She dipped it in some sauce and popped it in her mouth. She thought about the Suzuki that Aarni drove away in the day before. "It's one angle. Suicide makes it convenient, but if it was a forced confession that ended in suicide…"

"Or murder."

"Exactly." Petra took a sip of coke. "That's why they are examining the recording."

Maratse frowned. "If it was forced, then the suspect knew that Aarni Aviki had something to say."

"Or," Petra said, "he wanted Aviki to say something, and tortured him to make him say it."

"So, not Uutaaq."

"Obviously."

"So, we're back to Tukku, or some other man?"

"Or woman," Petra said, and then she put down her chopsticks, and smiled.

"What is it, Piitalaat?"

"I was thinking of Gaba. And what *I* thought about doing to him when I found out he was sleeping around."

"And?"

"We're forgetting someone."

"Malik's wife?"

"Exactly," Petra said. She picked up her chopsticks and fished after another king prawn. She skewered it and held it up in front of Maratse. "If you wanted to get back at your husband, if you hated him, what better way than getting him arrested for the murder of his rival's daughter."

"We don't know it's murder yet," Maratse said. He shifted his legs, and looked around the restaurant, nodding at one of the customers as he caught Maratse's eye. He looked at Petra. "Didn't the doctor's report confirm it was a boating accident?"

"An accident? Sure," Petra said. "Except, we both know that it wasn't."

"Hmm," Maratse said.

"Still, Naala Uutaaq, she must want to castrate her husband. That's what I wanted to do to Gaba. And if she could do it publicly…"

"*Iiji*, but would you torture another man to get at Gaba?"

"No," Petra said, the excitement in her voice evaporated. She plucked the prawn from the chopstick and chewed.

Maratse sipped his coke through the straw, thinking about the lengths to which a woman might go to get revenge on her husband, boyfriend, even a girlfriend. He had split up too many drunken fights, women fighting over the same lousy man, and a stabbing, when one woman killed another because she had heard something in town. Gossip, that led to murder. Jealousy was a powerful drug in Greenland, the kind that kept the police busy.

"Still," she said, "we should probably talk to her."

"Malik's wife?"

"Yes," Petra said. She shook her head. "Where did you go?"

"I was thinking," Maratse said. "You said Gaba was going to pick up Malik?"

"Yes, after the debate."

"The debate is tomorrow?"

"Yes." Petra frowned. "What are you thinking?"

"We can't wait to interview Malik, his wife, or Daniel Tukku."

"I know," Petra said. "But the Commissioner doesn't want to create a media storm if he has anyone picked up before the debate, or even right after it. We can't interfere."

"But Aviki's death should be enough for Malik Uutaaq to cancel the debate."

"Because Tinka's wasn't?"

"Obviously not. Nivi Winther is a strong woman." Maratse patted the pocket of his jacket, the one with the packet of cigarettes inside it. He looked at Petra. "Is Malik still popular?"

"Very. Even with the sympathy vote, it will be difficult for Nivi Winther to beat him in the debate." She tapped the ends of her chopsticks on the lid of the box. "Cancelling the debate is risky though, for both sides. It has to be for a good reason."

"Like a death, on both sides."

"Exactly," Petra said, and smiled. "I don't think I've ever heard you talk so much."

"Hmm," he said. "It's good to be working again." Maratse gritted his teeth and stood up; resting his hand on the back of the chair until he felt he was able to walk. "We have to pay and leave," he said.

"Where are we going?" Petra asked, and picked up her box of noodles.

"To Malik Uutaaq's house."

"We're going to talk to his wife?"

Maratse shook his head. "We're going to park outside, and wait."

"Why?"

"Because I think his life is in danger."

Petra's smartphone beeped with a text message as she paid for their meal. She looked at the screen and then handed the phone to Maratse. "It's the journalist. He wants a comment. Someone just sent him an email with a sound file attached."

Chapter 16

Saturday night chaos swirled around Malik Uutaaq, but he didn't notice. He was at home, sat in the armchair by the window, a large glass of gin in one hand, his smartphone in the other. Aarni's debate notes were on a small table to one side. Malik glanced at them once or twice as he dialled his communications chief for the fourth time, or was it the fifth? Malik couldn't remember. Nor could he remember when it was that Pipaluk started shouting, or why Naala had to shout back, something about her daughter acting as if they were rich, and that winter jackets, especially the *Canada Goose* label were not cheap. Malik heard the argument, he heard all the words, but he didn't listen. The debate was tomorrow, and his communications chief, the man he hired to be his shield and to tell him what to say and when to say it, had gone missing. Malik took another gulp of gin. The girl was dead. What did it matter that Pipaluk had lost her winter jacket?

"Malik," Naala said, and Malik realised she was standing in front of him.

"What?"

"Your son is in his room. You need to go and talk to him."

"I'm preparing for the debate. I haven't got time to talk to Sipu."

"No," she said and stabbed her finger towards his chest, "you're getting drunk." She snatched the bottle of gin from beneath his arm and held it up to the light, sloshing what little alcohol was left around the bottom of the bottle.

"Give me that." Malik dropped the smartphone

163

in his lap and reached for the bottle.

"Go and talk to your son."

"You mean *our* son."

"Right now? He's yours," Naala said and marched into the kitchen. She tipped the bottle over the sink and glared at her husband, daring him to say a single word.

Malik drank the last mouthful of gin from his glass and slapped it down on the coffee table as he walked out of the lounge, through the kitchen, and into the hall. He started to climb the stairs, stopping halfway to control his momentum, took a breath and continued onto the landing. Pipaluk looked out of her room and started to complain about her mother.

"Not now, princess," Malik said, as he walked past her room.

"But, dad," she called after him. "It's not fair. I didn't lose my jacket, or the other stuff, I left it hanging on the hook. It was *my* hook, dad. You should call the police or something."

Malik paused outside the door to Sipu's bedroom. He thought about the police, and wondered how he could explain to his daughter why that really wasn't a good idea. He opened the door and instantly wished that he had knocked first.

Sipu's room was dark but for the vivid pink and blue light emanating from the computer screen on his desk. He turned and fumbled for the mouse with one hand, as he tried to cover his crotch with the other. Malik stepped inside the room and quietly closed the door behind him.

"Sipu?"

"I'm sorry, dad," Sipu said. He closed one window on the screen with a click of the mouse, only to reveal another window, and a second and third cascading behind the first. All of them lurid. All of them graphic. Malik walked over to his son's desk, and turned the screen off.

"Pull your pyjamas up," Malik said.

He walked over to Sipu's bed and patted the mattress beside him. Sipu tugged his pyjama bottoms to his waist and crawled onto the bed. Malik curled his arm around his son, as Sipu buried his head in his father's armpit, his body jerking with small sobs.

"I'm not mad at you. You haven't done anything wrong. We just need to talk about it."

Malik felt the room spin around him, and he blinked to focus on the video game posters on the walls. None of them seemed willing to stop moving, so Malik closed his eyes. The room was warm. Malik lowered his head until his chin settled on his chest. He pictured the studio they were preparing for the debate at the cultural centre, the lights, the seats for the live audience, and the position of each of the three cameras. He had visited the studio with Aarni on the day of Tinka Winther's funeral. He had nodded with approval when the studio technicians had explained what they were doing, said *yes* to make-up and *no* to glasses. They showed him how the cordless microphone worked, and he remembered the light touch of the young woman who slipped the clasp of the microphone between his belt and the hem of his jeans. She was pretty. Not his type, but then his *type* seemed to get him into all kinds of trouble. Perhaps it was time to rethink his life?

Malik heard a snore and blinked his eyes open. Sipu had fallen asleep on his chest. He lifted his left hand to look at his watch, but it was too dark to see the hands. He didn't know if he had slept, or if his son's snoring had woken him, or was it the knock at the door. He squinted as a shaft of light from the landing lit Sipu's room as Naala opened the door and crept into the room. She looked at the window, and seemed to relax when she realised the curtains were drawn.

"Malik," she whispered.

"Naala? What is it?"

"Outside," she said. "There's a police car parked outside our house."

"What?" Malik sat up, peeled his son from his chest, and laid him down on the mattress, tugging the duvet over him as he stood up, walked to the window and reached for the curtain.

"Don't," Naala said. "They'll see you."

Malik stepped to one side of the window, and plucked at the edge of the curtain, just enough to see the police Toyota. The streetlights were on, but he couldn't see if anyone was inside the car. He let go of the curtain, and looked at his wife.

"I don't know," he said, but the twist of his guts suggested that he had an idea.

"Are you going to find out?"

"You want me to go and talk to them?"

"Yes," she said. "The police are outside our house, Malik. Yes, I want you to talk to them. What will the neighbours think?"

"Perhaps they are here for one of them?"

"Don't be an idiot," Naala said, and sighed.

They both turned as Pipaluk entered the room. She looked at her mother and then walked over to the window.

"Pipaluk, stop," Naala said.

"I want to see."

"It's nothing, princess," Malik said. "Go back to your room."

"If it's nothing," she said, "why are you whispering?"

"Your brother is asleep."

Pipaluk laughed, and said, "No, he's not, dad." She pointed at Sipu and he pulled the duvet over his head. "Faker," she said, and left the room.

Malik looked at his wife, as Pipaluk shut the door to her room and turned on her stereo. The music was loud enough to be heard, but not quite loud enough for them to tell her to turn it down. Naala beckoned for Malik to come with her, and they went down the stairs, and into the kitchen.

"This is because of you," she said, as Malik shut the kitchen door.

"How is this anything to do with me?"

"Because of *who* you are."

"The party leader of *Seqinnersoq*? Okay, maybe."

"And *what* you do," she said, and folded her arms across her chest.

"Politics?"

"Hah," she snorted, "is that what you call it?"

"Naala," Malik said, and pressed his palm to his forehead, "I don't want to fight anymore."

"No?"

"I'm tired. This last week has been…" He paused. "It's been difficult."

He looked at his wife, watched as the expression on her face softened, and her arms relaxed to her sides. She opened her mouth, as if she wanted to say something, and he wondered if he deserved to hear it, to hear soft words of encouragement, sympathy, and support, from the woman whose love he had betrayed time and time again. And then he saw her lips twitch, and any sympathy he might have received at his remorse was gone.

"You've had a difficult week? Oh, you poor love. How awful it must be to be you."

"Don't, Naala."

"Don't what, you bastard?" Naala jabbed her finger at the living room window, the one that faced out onto the street. "Go out there, and find out what the police are doing outside our house. Do that and I might just let you back in. Otherwise..." She paused to laugh. "Aarni Aviki."

Malik frowned. "What about him?"

"He told me to put up with you. That it was better to be the neglected wife of the First Minister of Greenland, than it was to be a divorced nobody. Can you believe that? He practically said that I should let you screw around, and that everything would be fine because we would have more money. He said that."

"He told me," Malik said, and glanced at the armchair where he had left his smartphone. Malik looked at his wife, and said, "Naala, do you want a divorce?"

The words didn't even surprise him. They just seemed to happen, pouring out together with the energy that was leaving his body, draining him on the eve of the most important day of his political campaign. If it was going to happen, he reasoned, why not make it now. What else could possibly go wrong?

Naala leaned back against the kitchen counter. She stared at her husband, as if he had started speaking a new language, as if he finally wanted to communicate. This second layer of vulnerability within the space of just a few minutes, actually stunned her, and she turned her back on Malik, not wanting to suggest one thing or another. Not yet. She gathered her thoughts, channelled them into words, and said, "Go outside. We'll talk after you've spoken to the police."

Malik waited for her to turn around. When he realised she wasn't going to, he walked out of the kitchen, shut the door quietly behind him, and put on a pair of shoes. He chose a jacket from the rack and left the house. The walk across the street was twice as long as he remembered, and he wondered how much gin he had drunk before Naala tipped the remains of the bottle down the sink. He stopped within half a metre of the police car, wiped a mist of rain from his face, and peered in through the driver's window. Malik waited.

Petra pressed the button in the door to lower the window, and looked at Malik. She nodded and waited for him to speak.

"You look familiar," he said.

"Sergeant Jensen. I'm working on the Tinka Winther case."

"Is that why you're here, outside my house?" He waited as Petra turned to look at the man sitting next to her. Malik took a step closer and peered into the interior. "I don't know you."

"My name is Maratse."

"And you're working the case too?" Malik shook his head. "Two police officers, outside my house, on a Saturday night. Is that really the best use of police resources? I'm sure there are plenty of drunks you could pick up in town."

Petra sighed. "My shift finished an hour ago."

"Really?"

"And I'm not a police officer," Maratse said, and opened the passenger door.

Malik watched him as he took a long time to walk around the front of the car. "Then what are you doing here? Is this some form of harassment?"

"I really wish it was," Petra said. She shot a sharp look at Maratse as he leaned against the side of the car.

"Then one of you had better explain, before I call the Commissioner."

"You don't need to do that, Malik," Maratse said. "I just want to talk."

Petra stifled a laugh, as Malik looked at them both. "My *friend* has recently developed a chatty streak," she said.

"Piitalaat," Maratse said. "Please…"

"No, David," Petra said. She gripped the wheel. "I don't agree with you on this, and," she said, and looked at Malik, "I don't even want to be here."

Malik wiped the rain from his face. He blinked, as he tried to make sense of the conversation. He glanced over his shoulder at his house, almost wishing he was back in the kitchen, arguing with Naala. "What is this? It's like the good cop, bad cop scenario, except neither of you seems to know who is playing who. Why don't I leave you to it? I mean, if you want to figure out your problems, that's fine. I have plenty of my own."

"My friend is angry with me for making her come here tonight," Maratse said.

"I can see that. Why is that my problem?"

"You are a problem, and you have problems."

Maratse lit a cigarette, and rolled it into the gap between his teeth. "You are a problem because your politics suggest my friend is not a true Greenlander." Maratse considered switching to Greenlandic, but continued in Danish. "She thinks you are splitting the country, and I agree with her. But that's not why we are here tonight."

"No? Good, because that would be harassment."

"We're here," Petra said, "because my friend is worried about you. He thinks you might do something stupid, or that someone might do something to you."

"Like what? What are we talking about? Why would I do anything stupid?"

"When did you last speak with Aarni Aviki?" Maratse asked.

"Early this morning. Why?"

"He has had a difficult day."

"Has something happened to Aarni?" Malik looked at Petra. "Tell me."

Petra bit her lip, as she thought about what to say. "He committed suicide."

"What?" Malik looked at Maratse. "What did she say?"

"We found his body a few hours ago," Petra said, and glanced at the house. "Is your wife home?"

"Yes," Malik said. He jerked his hands; palms open, and said, "My wife, my kids, everyone's home. Why?"

"That's good," Maratse said. "We're going to stay out here tonight. Perhaps you should get a good night's sleep, prepare for your debate."

"We're sorry about Mr Aviki," Petra said. "Get some rest."

Malik took a step backwards, staring at Maratse and Petra, confused by what they said. Naala met him at the front door, peering around his shoulder at the police car.

"What do they want?"

"They want to make sure I am okay."

"Are they going to stay there all night?"

"Yes." Malik reached out for Naala's hand. "Aarni's dead, Naala."

"What?"

"Suicide. They just told me."

"And that's why they are here?"

"Maybe. I don't know. I think they are protecting me."

"Malik," Naala said, "do you need protection?"

"I don't know."

Sapaat

SUNDAY

Chapter 17

Nivi Winther smiled at her secretary and signed three documents ready to be actioned after the weekend. The secretary paused, hovering at Nivi's desk until the First Minister looked up from her laptop screen. The look on her secretary's face suggested she wanted to express her sympathy for Nivi's loss, the third person to do so this morning, and likely not the last.

"Is everything all right, Bibi?"

"Yes, I just wanted to say…" Bibi paused, clutching the documents to her chest. "I wanted to say how sorry I am, about Tinka."

"It's kind of you to say so," Nivi said.

"If there's anything I can do."

"I'll be sure to ask." Nivi smiled and waited for Bibi to leave the room. She nodded when Bibi asked if she should close the door.

A moment's peace, that's what Nivi wanted most. As the door closed with a click, she leaned back in her chair and closed her eyes. She thought of Tinka's grave, looking out onto the icebergs in Uummannaq fjord. She could almost feel the cold breath of ice on her cheeks, freezing everything in its path, including the tears on her cheeks. Nivi realised she was crying, and opened her eyes. She brushed the tears from her face with her finger, and then swore when she realised her mascara would need fixing, again. It was going to be a long day.

Nivi searched for a distraction, picked her smartphone up from the desk, and called Maratse. She smiled as he answered, in the hope of portraying a positive vibe to hide her moment of sadness. "I just wanted to check-in," she said.

"*Iji.*"

"Is everything all right? Any news?"

"Nothing yet."

"You're sure?" Nivi looked up as Daniel tapped on the glass in the door. She waved him in. "You sound tired, Constable."

"Everything is all right," Maratse said.

Nivi thanked him, ended the call with a tap of her thumb, and put her phone down. She waved at the chair in front of her desk and waited for Daniel to sit down.

"Constable?" he said. "I thought Sergeant Jensen was handling the case?"

"She is," Nivi said. "I just asked for a little more help."

"Asked? You mean you talked with the Commissioner? Nivi," Daniel said, "that could be seen as abusing police resources. What did the official report say?"

"You know what it said, Daniel."

"An accident." Daniel gestured with his hand. "Tinka's death was an accident. Albeit with a lot of unanswered questions, I understand." He stopped when he noticed Nivi's eyes. "I'm sorry," he said. "You've been crying. That was insensitive of me."

"It's all right, Daniel. I will cry a lot more before I am ready to move on."

"Then, perhaps we should discuss it again."

"It?" Nivi shook her head. "I'm going to the debate. I told you that the first time, the second, and the third. I don't want to talk about it again. That's final."

"Fine. I understand."

"Do you?"

"Of course," Daniel said. "The country needs to see you. They need to feel as though you can lead them, even in times of sorrow. But the funeral was on Friday, Nivi. It's too soon. There's a chance the people will think you are too strong. They might even think you are insensitive."

"If we cancel the debate, Malik Uutaaq wins. You said so."

"We don't have to cancel. There is an alternative."

"Ah, now we come to it." Nivi pushed back her chair and stood up. She walked to the window and leaned against the sill. "You want your moment, don't you, Daniel." She laughed. "And you call me insensitive?"

"It's the right thing to do," he said.

"For you, perhaps. But what about the party? Are you going to debate the politics of language with Malik Uutaaq? And turn the whole evening into a popularity contest. Because if you do, we will lose. Do you understand that?"

"Language is not the only topic for debate."

"It is for Malik Uutaaq."

"I've done a deal with Aarni Aviki. They're willing to debate everything."

"Really?"

"Yes."

"And what did you give away?"

"Nothing."

"I see." Nivi folded her arms. "Then what did you threaten him with?"

Daniel looked away for a moment. "I said I would go to the press."

"With what?" It hit Nivi a second later, and she

didn't know if she should be angry or disgusted. "You used Tinka, didn't you?"

"I used what I had." Daniel recoiled in his chair as Nivi took a step towards him.

"I told you I didn't want that article out there." Nivi reached for her phone. "I told you that."

"Who are you calling?"

"The journalist."

"He's deaf, Nivi."

"I'll text him."

"You don't have to. He had nothing to do with it."

"Then tell me what you said to Aviki."

Daniel smoothed his hands on his trousers, steepled his fingers beneath his chin, and looked at Nivi. She tucked the phone into the crook of her arm, and waited.

"I told him we could confirm that Malik was with Tinka at a party before she died."

"And can we? Can we confirm that?"

"Does it matter?"

"It matters, Daniel," Nivi said, her voice rising, "because in just a few hours I will be standing next to a man who might have been the last person to see my daughter alive. He might even…" Nivi started to tremble.

"Yes?"

She lowered her voice, took a breath. "He might even have been responsible for her death somehow. He might even have killed her."

Daniel stood up and put his arm around Nivi's shoulders. He pulled her close, until her head was on his chest. Nivi closed her fist around her phone and leaned into Daniel's body. She trembled, and he held her tight.

"That's why," he whispered, "it should be me doing the debate, Nivi."

"No," she said, her voice muffled by his body.

"Think about it. Rest. Then we'll talk."

Daniel walked Nivi out of her office and down the hall to a lounge with a coffee machine and two long sofas. He guided Nivi onto the sofa furthest from the door, prised the phone from her hand, and placed it on the coffee table. There was a blanket at the far end of the sofa, and he tugged it over her body as she lifted her feet and laid her head on the pillow.

"Don't let me sleep too long," she said, as Daniel walked to the door and turned off the lights.

"I won't," he said, and closed the door.

Nivi let herself drift back to the icebergs in the fjord, as she watched Tinka run along a sandy beach, chasing the spumes of mist from the whales as they surfaced far out in the depths of the fjord. Life was simpler in the north, and harsher. Help, of any kind, was further away. Families had to provide for one another, and rivalry, no matter how strong, and for whatever the reason, had to be overcome, especially now, at the onset of winter.

She woke when Bibi whispered that it was time for her to wake up. Nivi smelled fresh coffee, and wiped her eyes as she sat up and pulled the blanket to one side. She reached for the coffee on the table, and took a bite of the bread and cheese that Bibi had prepared.

"I thought Daniel would wake me," she said.

"He asked me to."

"Where is he?"

"At Katuaq, getting ready for the debate."

Nivi bit back a remark and took another deliberate sip of coffee. She couldn't recall when Daniel had begun to make his play for her position, but she realised she wasn't surprised, just angry that he had chosen to use Tinka as leverage.

"Okay," she said. "Did he leave a message?"

"No," Bibi said, and shook her head. Nivi noticed the twitch of the muscle in the young woman's cheek, but decided not to press her.

"Thank you for the coffee," Nivi said, and stood up. "I'll just freshen up, and then we can walk to Katuaq together."

"Yes, First Minister," Bibi said.

Bibi tidied away the coffee and remains of Nivi's sandwich as Nivi used the bathroom. When Nivi came out, Bibi was dressed for the rain, and had Nivi's jacket over one arm, and her smartphone in her hand.

"I'll need my notes," Nivi said, and took a step towards her office.

"I have them here." Bibi turned to reveal Nivi's bag hanging from her shoulder.

"You've thought of everything."

"Yes," Bibi said, and beamed. "I just want to help."

"And on a Sunday, too. *Qujanaq.*"

Nivi put on her jacket, slipped her phone into her pocket, and slung her bag over one shoulder. Bibi walked with her to the door, and they braved a deluge of rain as they hurried across the car park to the entrance of the Katuaq Cultural Centre. They slipped inside and shook the rain from their jackets, invigorated at the blast of fresh air they had just received. Bibi took Nivi's jacket, and said she would wait for her behind the cameras. As she walked away, Nivi caught a glimpse of Maratse sitting at a table in the café by the entrance.

"We're ready for you, First Minister," said a woman from the television studio.

"Just a minute," Nivi said, and walked over to Maratse. "Constable," she said, "it's good to see you." Maratse stood up, and shook Nivi's hand. "You're alone?"

"Sergeant Jensen is inside," he said. "In the audience."

"I see. And you're not coming inside?"

"I don't like politics," he said.

"Constable," she said, and leaned in closer to Maratse. "I want you in the audience. I want you to watch Malik Uutaaq."

"He's no danger to you. And Gaba Alatak is here to provide security."

"I'm not paying you to be my bodyguard, Constable," Nivi said, and checked the irritation in her voice. "I just want you to observe Uutaaq, as part of your investigation."

"I'm not worried about him."

"Well," Nivi said, as the studio assistant called her name, "perhaps you should be."

Nivi strode away from Maratse, and followed the woman from the studio all the way to the temporary make-up room squeezed into a corner of the space behind the stage. Nivi could hear the audience being seated as she sat down and closed her eyes. The light brush of powder on her cheeks tickled, and she focussed on it, calming her nerves and finding a space in her mind within which she could function. Somewhere she had a semblance of control, no matter what forces pulled at her from the outside.

The sense of calm diminished at the sound of a quiet cough to her right. She opened her eyes and saw Daniel standing next to the tall police officer she recognised as the leader of the SRU.

"You forgot to wake me, Daniel," she said.

"I thought it best you get as much rest as possible," he said.

"I bet you did." Nivi looked at Gaba. "Sergeant Alatak. What can I do for you?"

"I want to give you some advance warning, before the debate."

"About what?"

"Excuse me," Daniel said to the make-up assistant, "can you give us some privacy?" The woman nodded, placed her brush on the table, and walked away. Nivi noticed that Daniel was also wearing a light brush of powder on his cheeks. They made eye contact and he retreated a step, nodding at Gaba that he should continue.

"There's been a development in the investigation," Gaba said, "and I am ready to bring Malik Uutaaq down to the station for questioning."

"You're going to arrest him?" Nivi asked.

"I'm going to bring him in," Gaba said.

"That's different?"

"Nivi," Daniel said, "there's something more. The police found Aarni Aviki last night. He committed suicide, and there was a Dictaphone in his pocket."

"What?" Nivi frowned. This was moving too fast.

"The tape confirms that Malik Uutaaq was with your daughter, and that Aarni knew it all along." Daniel paused to swap a look with Gaba. He looked at Nivi. "Maybe now you'll agree that it is best that I do the debate. I mean, it's clear," he said, and placed his hand on her shoulder, "you're in shock. It's understandable. Anyone would be."

"No," Nivi said, "I have to do this. For Tinka." She tried to stand, but Daniel increased the pressure on her shoulder, just enough to push her back down onto the chair.

"Tinka is the reason you shouldn't do this. The police want to question Malik Uutaaq in connection with her murder…"

"I didn't say that," Gaba said.

"I know," Daniel said and let go of Nivi's shoulder. "But still, it's likely he was involved somehow."

"I didn't say that either."

"Excuse me, Sergeant Alatak," Daniel said. "Can you give the First Minister and me a moment?" Daniel waited until Gaba retreated to the shadows beside the stage entrance. "Think about it, Nivi. This is an important event. It could decide the outcome of the election. Can you honestly look at Malik Uutaaq without seeing the face of Tinka's murderer?"

"I…" Nivi started to speak, but Daniel interrupted, his voice a harsh whisper.

"Think about it, carefully. This man slept with Tinka…"

"Daniel stop," Nivi said and lifted her hand, pushing at his face as he leaned closer.

"… he put her in a boat, and he sailed all the way north…"

"Daniel…"

"All the way to Inussuk, so he could kill her right in front of your childhood home."

"You don't know that," she said, her voice trembling, tears glistening on her powdered cheeks. Nivi wiped at them as Gaba walked over. "I'm all right," she said, as he put his hand on Daniel's chest, and pushed him away from her.

"I'll do the debate," Daniel said, as he brushed free of Gaba's grip. "You need to rest, Nivi."

And there it was, her way out. Daniel could stand in for her, and she wouldn't need to be strong for Greenland, or even for Tinka. No one would think any less of her. She had buried her daughter just a matter of hours ago. It was perfectly normal. Understandable. She could walk away, and she almost did.

How far would you go, mum?

Nivi shook a little as she looked up, convinced it was Tinka's voice she had just heard. But, of course, it couldn't be. The question, however, was valid.

"How far would I go?" Nivi whispered. She caught the quizzical look on Daniel's face, and she repeated the question, changing it ever so slightly to say, "How far do you want me to go?"

"I don't understand," he said.

"Don't you?" Nivi almost laughed. She wiped her cheeks with the back of her hand and waved for the make-up assistant to come over. "Malik Uutaaq might be a monster," she said, "but he's innocent until proven guilty. Right now, the only thing he is guilty of doing is causing a rift between the people of this country. I can stop him. For Tinka, and for all the young men and women, mothers and fathers like her, the ones who call Greenland home." Nivi took a long breath and a long look at Daniel. "You're right about one thing, Daniel. I am in shock. But so is the country, and it is time to do something about it."

Nivi sat down and closed her eyes as the assistant applied a new brush of powder to her cheeks. When she opened her eyes again, Daniel was gone. She heard the audience fidget at the arrival of Malik Uutaaq, and she opened her eyes.

"I'm ready," she said.

Chapter 18

From his table in the café Maratse had a good view of the guests as they arrived. He saw Malik Uutaaq and his wife walk through the main entrance. Naala pointed at Maratse, but Malik took her arm and led her into the auditorium. They had been gone less than ten minutes when he heard raised voices coming from the studio, followed by a crash of wood, and what could have been a camera toppling over.

"What's going on?" he said, as Petra darted out of the auditorium.

"It's Uutaaq," Petra said. "He's running away."

Petra grabbed Maratse by the arm and dragged him in the direction of the cloakroom and toilets at the far end of the cultural centre, past the main auditorium. Maratse grunted at the pain, found a rhythm, and picked up speed. The smell of rain on the wind blustered through the emergency exit, as the door swept back and forth across the slight concrete ramp that merged with the gravel and stones of Nuuk's untamed surfaces. Petra stopped, her hand shielding her eyes from the rain as she searched for signs of the pursuit.

"He came this way," she said.

"What happened?" Maratse slowed to a halt beside her. His legs palsied for a moment, before the pain was renewed and he bit down on this tongue and worked hard to control his breathing.

"Malik was on his way to the podium, and then Daniel Tukku came onto the stage, looking pretty pissed-off," Petra said. She stopped when she saw Maratse biting back the pain, but he urged her to continue with a wave of his hand. "From where I was sitting, I saw Daniel shake Malik's hand, and then he leaned in close to say something in Malik's ear. After that, Malik recoiled, ripped his hand free of Daniel's, and ran for the exit."

"And Daniel?"

"He did his best to look bewildered, but I'm sure I saw him hide a smirk behind his hand. Miki, one of Gaba's team, pushed through the crowd from the back of the room, and Gaba was on Malik's heels, from the moment he started to run." Petra took a step closer to Maratse, dipped her head to look at his face, and sighed when he smiled. "How about I get a car?"

"That would be good," he said.

Petra ran back inside as Maratse walked across the rough ground behind the centre to the road. He blinked in the flash of blue lights, as Petra slewed the police Toyota to a stop at the curb. Maratse walked around the front of the car and climbed in. Petra accelerated towards the town centre as Maratse buckled his seatbelt. The radio in the centre of the dashboard chattered with updates and positive sightings. Gaba's voice burst through the static as he gave directions. Malik had just run inside Hotel Hans Egede.

Petra turned on the siren and stomped on the accelerator. Maratse glanced at her face, resisting the temptation to smile at the concentration evident in the way she pressed her lips flat, ignoring the loose strands of wet hair clinging to her forehead and cheeks. Petra swung a hard right onto the road running through the centre of Nuuk. She braked outside the main entrance to the hotel, and rolled the window down.

"Go around, to the rear," Miki shouted from the steps. Maratse noted he had his hand on the grip of his pistol.

Petra acknowledged Miki with a nod, jerked the Toyota into first gear and then braked as a second patrol car shot between the row of taxis parked alongside the pavement. She swore, and then followed the police car through the gap passing beneath the first floor of the hotel.

Maratse reached out and squeezed Petra's arm. "Easy," he said.

"Right." Petra slowed the Toyota to a crawl as they drove past Gaba. He waved them on, and then they heard his voice on the radio, telling all those involved in the search that he was going back inside the hotel.

"He might have doubled back," he said. "Put a car at the end of the road, near the gym."

"That's us," Petra said, as she grabbed the radio and told everyone she was taking that position. Petra roared up the road as the other police car turned and headed back towards the hotel. Petra turned in the gravel parking area of the cross-fit gym and pointed the Toyota back towards the hotel. She switched off the emergency lights and took a breath. A few seconds later she turned the engine off and Maratse looked up as the rain drummed on the roof.

"Why would he run? Where would he go?"

"That's two questions," Maratse said.

"All right, pick one."

"He ran because Daniel told him to."

"Because Gaba was there to pick him up?"

"*Iji.*"

"And where? Where would he go? Unless he

187

went to the docks, there's no way out of Nuuk. Unless you climb over the mountains."

Maratse sighed at the thought. The pain in his legs had become tolerable when walking, but irregular movement such as running spiralled the pain through his nerves. The thought of climbing mountains was unbearable. He chose to think instead.

"So, he's running because he's guilty?" Petra said, as she peered down the dark street.

"Of what?"

"Sleeping with Tinka Winther."

"Tinka was seventeen. It's not a crime."

"If he forced her."

"We don't know that he did. The only thing that connects Malik with Tinka is his daughter's winter jacket."

"That's enough to begin with." Petra looked at Maratse for a moment, the lights of the radio reflected in her eyes. "I thought you were on my side?"

"I don't understand."

"That man, everything he stands for, is driving a wedge between the people of this country, even between me and my friends, and now you."

"I am still your friend, Piitalaat."

"But you are on his side."

"No," Maratse said. "I just don't think he killed Tinka."

Gaba's voice burst through the speakers of the radio, a little out of breath, but triumphant. Malik was in custody, and on his way back to the station.

"That's it then," Petra said, and started the car. "We'll soon find out."

"Will Gaba do the interview?" Maratse asked.

"Initially, yes."

"Then drop me off at Nivi's office."

"Okay," Petra said. She pulled onto the road and drove at a sedate pace past the hotel, across the main road, past the police station and around the back of the government building. She parked and turned off the engine.

"You're coming with me?" Maratse asked, as he unbuckled his belt and opened the passenger door.

"Yes," she said. "It's been a long night, and another long day. It will feel good to tell her we have taken Malik into custody. It might even help her relax."

Maratse followed Petra to the main doors. They buzzed to be let in, and then waved at a cleaner mopping the floor. He opened the door, and said he was the only one in the building.

"The lights are lit on the second floor," Petra said. "Mind if we go and look?" The cleaner shook his head and Petra led Maratse to the elevator. "It is Sunday," she said, as the doors closed.

They got out on the second floor and walked towards Nivi's office. There was a shadow of movement in the office next to hers, and Maratse recognised Nivi's secretary. She bumped into them as she walked out of the office into the corridor.

"I'm sorry," she said. She looked at their black jackets, and covered her mouth with her hand. "Has something happened?"

"We were just coming to see the First Minister," Petra said. "Is she here?"

Bibi shook her head. She looked at Maratse. "We came here after the commotion in the auditorium. She rested for a short while on the sofa, and then

Daniel came over."

"Where did she go then?"

"He took her home."

"Okay," Petra said, as Maratse pulled his mobile out of his pocket. He studied the screen for a second, opened the list of contacts and used the cursor to click Nivi's name. Petra waited as he held the mobile to his ear, but Nivi didn't answer. "I'll try Daniel," she said. Maratse nodded and took Bibi to one side as Petra dialled.

"How was she when Daniel arrived?"

"She was angry. She thinks he said something to Malik Uutaaq."

"And what did he say to that?"

"He said the debate was over, that the police were talking to Malik, and that there was nothing more they could do today. He said something about getting ready for the media on Monday."

"Tomorrow."

"Yes."

Petra slipped her smartphone into her pocket, and shook her head. "He's not answering either."

"Bibi," Maratse said, "where does Daniel live?"

"In Qinngorput. One of the new apartments."

"Which block?" asked Petra.

"Five."

Petra nodded at Maratse, and they started to walk towards the elevators.

"Is everything all right?" Bibi called after them.

"*Iiji*," Maratse said. "Go home. It's been a long day." He waved as they entered the elevator.

"Why Daniel's apartment?" Petra asked, as they walked out of the building and got in the car. "Shouldn't we go to Nivi's house? That's where Bibi said he was taking her." She started the car and began driving towards the new area of Nuuk called Qinngorput.

Maratse stretched his legs and then glanced at the clock on the dashboard. "Faster, Piitalaat."

Petra turned on the emergency lights and the siren. She buckled her belt with one hand. "Back-up?" she said, and reached for the radio.

"*Iiji*," Maratse said. He slid his arm into the handle in the door panel, as Petra called for assistance, and accelerated. She weaved the Toyota in and out of the light traffic heading out of the centre, slowed as a bus pulled out, and then gunned the Toyota past the bus and up the hill. Maratse tried calling Nivi a second time, stuffing the mobile back in his pocket when she didn't answer.

"It could be nothing," Petra said, as she braked into the curve of a roundabout, and accelerated out of it. The rain drummed on the roof and splashed from the bonnet onto the windscreen. Petra turned the wipers on full, and concentrated on the road as it dipped past the turning to the airport. The apartment towers of Qinngorput were visible across the black water of the fjord as Petra sped up the hill. She glanced at the rear view mirror, as a flash of blue lights caught her eye.

"Maybe," Maratse said.

"But you don't think so?"

"I think Daniel has worked hard to make sure everything points at Malik Uutaaq."

"If you're right, then he doesn't need to do anymore."

"If I'm right," Maratse said, and looked at Petra, "he's just getting started."

"I'm not sure I follow…" Petra's words caught in her throat, as a black American import clipped the driver's side of the Toyota, forcing them off the road and into a wall of granite through which the road had been cut. Petra gasped as the front end of the Toyota crumpled and the rear wheels lifted on impact. The engine stalled as the back end of the car bounced back onto the road and the black car disappeared down the hill and into the night.

"Piitalaat," Maratse said, as he tried to release the seatbelt clamping him to the passenger seat. He reached out to touch Petra; her head was slumped on her chest, and blood trickled from her nose. The siren of the police car they had called for back-up wailed as it crested the rise of the hill. The Toyota skidded to a stop in the gravel beside them. The policeman in the passenger seat leaped out of the car and ran towards them, as the driver backed up and positioned the police car in the road, lights flashing. The siren stopped as the policeman opened Petra's door.

"Are you hurt?"

"I'm okay," Petra said, the words slurring out of her mouth. "Did you see him?"

"Who?"

"The car that hit us," Maratse said. "A large American car. Black."

"We didn't see it happen. You were just on the other side of the hill." The policeman looked at his partner as he jogged over to Maratse's side of the crumpled Toyota. "Did you see a black import?"

"Yeah, it passed us just as we were coming up the hill."

"Did you happen to see the driver?" Petra asked.

"Not clearly. But it was a male."

"Was there a passenger?" Maratse asked, as the man cut him free of the belt pinning him to the seat.

"Yes. Female, maybe. It was dark," he said, and helped Maratse out of the car.

"Get on the radio, and put out the description of the car," Petra said, as the policeman walked her away from the car and over to the rock wall by the side of the road. "And," she said, as the policeman encouraged her to sit, "we need to find Daniel Tukku and Nivi Winther."

"The First Minister?"

"Yes, the First Minister," Petra said. She nodded as the policeman took a step back and made the call on his radio. She closed her eyes when she heard the static response that his request had been received and broadcasted.

"I need to stand," Maratse said, as the policeman walked him over to where Petra was sitting.

"Sure, go ahead. We'll have an ambulance here any minute."

Petra held up her hand and Maratse took it. She leaned her head back and looked at him. "What were you saying? Something about him just getting started?"

"Daniel?"

"Yes."

"He's the only one to gain from any of this."

"What do you mean?"

"If Malik is revealed to be a hypocrite... because of his affair with Tinka Winther..."

"*Seqinnersoq* loses the popular vote."

"He can't take the risk that Tinka would say it wasn't Malik she was seeing. So he kills her, and frames Malik by dressing Tinka in the jacket..."

"That belongs to Malik's daughter." Maratse squeezed Petra's hand. He let go and bit his lip as he sat down.

"I thought it was better to stand?"

"But I am getting dizzy," he said, and sat down beside Petra.

"Everything changed with Aviki's suicide tape. It was very convenient." Petra looked at Maratse. "You don't think it was suicide, do you?"

"*Eeqqi.*" Maratse shook his head.

"You think Daniel forced him to make the link between Malik and Tinka?"

Maratse nodded. "And it was a mistake. He didn't think it through, but he enjoyed it. Maybe even more than what he did to Tinka. It got the better of him."

"*If* he killed her. We don't know for sure. There's no evidence."

"Which is why we need to find him. He might have discredited Malik, but Nivi could still lead the country."

"And Daniel needs her out of the way, if he is going to have any kind of power."

"*Iiji.*"

Petra wiped a clot from her nose, and then pressed her hand beneath it to stem the flow of more blood. She swore and squirmed her hand into her jacket pocket for a tissue. The rain soaked into the packet as she wrestled one free, pressing the soggy mess of paper against her nose.

"This is hopeless," she said.

A siren wailed up the hill as an ambulance stopped beside the two police cars. The paramedics walked over to assess Petra's injuries, checking Maratse a moment later. Petra called to the policemen.

"I need one of you to call the Commissioner. Ask him to meet us at the hospital."

"Is that necessary? It's Sunday night, Sergeant."

"Didn't you hear what I said about the First Minister?"

"Yes…"

Petra stared at him as the paramedics helped her onto a stretcher. The man nodded, and grabbed his radio.

Chapter 19

Just as Daniel coasted to a stop in the black Dodge RAM, the sodium lamp above the fishing trawler that was idling at the far end of the quay extinguished with a soft thump. He turned off the engine and leaned over the handbrake to tighten the knot of rope binding Nivi Winther's wrists. He winked at her as she followed his every move, her gaze glued to his face. He reached up and tugged at a corner of the duct tape covering her mouth. It was still secure. Daniel leaned back in his seat and tapped a beat on the steering wheel, rising in tempo as a crewman from the trawler walked down the gangplank and onto the quay. The crewman stared through the windscreen, first at Daniel, and then at his passenger. Daniel waved and lowered the driver's window.

"Everything all right?" he asked.

"We're ready to go," the man said. He looked at Nivi and lowered his voice. "Will this come back to us?"

"No," Daniel said, "of course not."

"I'm not so sure."

"I will take care of it," Daniel said. "Just get me to Ilulissat."

The crewman looked at his watch. "The captain says we'll be there before dawn, if we go now."

"Then let's go," Daniel said, and opened the door. He jogged around the front of the big American car, and made a theatrical bow before opening the passenger door. "First Minister," he said and reached over to unbuckle her seatbelt, "your cruise starts now. If you would be so kind as to…"

Nivi kicked Daniel in the knee as he pulled her

out of the passenger seat. He buckled and she aimed another kick at his body, but her leg bounced off his side, and she stumbled. Nivi's smartphone skittered onto the quay, as Daniel recovered. He grimaced as he marched past Nivi to pick up her phone. He tossed it over the side, the tiny splash of water barely audible, as he grabbed Nivi by the arm and dragged her up the gangplank and onto the deck of the trawler.

"Hey," the crewman called out from the quay, "what about the car?"

"It's not mine," Daniel said. He opened the door to the wheelhouse, pulled Nivi up the short ladder and thrust her onto the bench. Nivi's coat caught on the corner of the table and he wrenched it free. The captain turned at the commotion and tensed at the sight of Nivi.

"Is that who I think it is?" he said, his voice coarse like the seabed.

"Yes," Daniel said. He slapped at the dirt on his trousers and looked at the captain. "What? Is there a problem?"

"There could be."

"Only if you don't get a move on. Listen," Daniel said, "if you want us off your boat before it gets light. I suggest you get going." He turned at the sound of the crewman drawing the gangplank onboard the trawler. "He has the right idea."

"You never said it would be her."

"That's right, I didn't." Daniel waved his hand at Nivi. "I ask you again. Do we have a problem?"

"No."

"And the money?"

"Now the money makes sense." The captain

turned on the trawler's lights and the crewman on the deck looked up at the wheelhouse, shielding his eyes with his hand. The captain opened a window and gave the order to cast off the ropes.

The diesel engines vibrated through the deck as the captain reversed a short distance, before levering the trawler into gear and pulling away from the quay. Daniel pressed his face against the window as they passed two more fishing trawlers and an adventure cruise ship pushing the limits of the Greenland sailing season. He started to relax as the captain pulled away from Nuuk and increased speed. If the weather did not change drastically, as it often did in Greenland, Daniel knew that they would make good time along the coast, and that his own modest powerboat would have no problems sailing north from Ilulissat and around the Uummannaq peninsula. The First Minister didn't know it yet, but he was taking her home, to see her daughter.

Daniel sat down beside Nivi as the captain changed the interior lighting to a red glow, and the crewman entered the wheelhouse.

"Everything's stowed," he said to the captain. He ignored the passengers.

"Good." The captain pointed at the coffee machine. "Make a fresh pot, and then go below. I'll call you when I want to be relieved."

"Right, boss."

Daniel leaned close to Nivi as the crewman prepared the coffee. He whispered in her ear, "You might want to rest. It's been a busy day, and you have another long day ahead of you tomorrow." He kicked off his shoes and stretched his legs beneath the table, propping his feet up on the opposite bench. The trawler rose over a gentle wave as they cleared the mouth of the fjord. Daniel waited for the crewman to go below and then closed his eyes.

Nivi fidgeted beside Daniel, but he did his best to ignore her. He had given her every opportunity to take a step back, to take it easy. But she had chosen to make life difficult. He teased at the thought as he clicked through his actions over the past week. Everything was fitting into place, exactly as he had imagined it would. He had planned every move, every detail, all the way back to the last day of the school term in June, before they broke up for the long summer holiday. Daniel almost smiled at the ease with which he had walked into the school and picked up Pipaluk Uutaaq's winter clothes, carrying them over his arm like any other parent.

The trawler lifted over the crest of another shallow wave. Daniel opened one eye, watched the captain as he casually sipped at his coffee, and then glanced at Nivi, who was wide-eyed, frantic.

"Go to sleep," he said, and closed his eyes.

His masterstroke, he felt, was Aarni Aviki's suicide. It had been difficult to wait until Tinka Winther's body had been found to make the connection between Uutaaq and her death. There had been a time, he recalled, when he had worried that she would never be found. And so, he had to put Aarni Aviki in the spotlight, and a suicide note was the perfect solution, perhaps the only solution.

Of course, the irony was not lost on Daniel Tukku. All this work, all this effort, his *machinations* as he liked to call them, was ultimately going to be for nothing. Any success he might have achieved, any power he might have gained, was lost the moment he abducted Greenland's First Minister. He could sense a feeling of regret. But that regret was easily matched with the feeling of power far sweeter than political leadership, the power over life itself.

He opened his eyes and looked at Nivi, searching for the fear that flickered across her cheeks in tiny muscle twitches. He felt aroused, all of a sudden, even at the tiny blister of red skin tracing the edges of the tape sealing her mouth. An allergic reaction, perhaps. He lowered his gaze to look at her hands, titillating himself at the sight of the blush of irritation where the rope scratched at her wrists. He looked at her eyes last, and was almost lost in the exhilaration that rushed through his body at the sight of pure, naked fear, the terror of not knowing one's fate.

He knew then that he could not sleep. But he would close his eyes, because there, in the darkness, he could replay and rerun his first exploration of true power, when he pinned and penetrated Nivi's daughter in the fear-stoked cabin of his motorboat. And soon, he realised, he would do it all over again, with the mother.

Such thoughts, replayed over and over, entertained Daniel all the way up the coast from Nuuk to Ilulissat, and it was only when the captain shook his arm that he realised they had arrived. Everything was going to plan. He was but minutes away from satisfaction, and he intended to enjoy it. But the gun in the captain's hand confused him, and he was suddenly alert.

"What's this?"

"A handgun," the captain said. "Empty, of course, but," he said, and shrugged, "I just wanted you to see it."

"It's illegal to have a handgun in Greenland," Daniel said, and took the gun when the captain offered it to him.

"Yes," the captain said, with a nod at Nivi, "but then, present circumstances…"

Daniel raised his eyebrows and handed the gun back to the captain. "It's nice."

"It's insurance." The captain slid a pen through the trigger guard and dropped the gun inside a plastic bag.

"Wait," Daniel said. He looked at the captain, and then at the long fillet knife in the crewman's hands, as he climbed up the ladder and into the wheelhouse. "What are you doing?"

"You haven't paid us yet," the captain said. He jerked his thumb over his shoulder in the direction of the Ilulissat marina. The sky was a hazy blue and pink as the sun strained at the limits of its early winter zenith, lighting the snow-clad mountains as it began a slow circle on a low horizon.

"I have the money on my boat. Take me there, and I will pay you. Just as we agreed."

The captain nodded at the crewman and crossed the wheelhouse floor to steer the boat the last hundred metres inside the marina. "Where's your boat?" he asked

"It should be alongside the quay. I paid extra to have it moored close to where you can pull alongside." Daniel stood up and walked to the stand next to the captain. "There," he said, and pointed at a large motorboat with a lighting flash painted on the hull. He glanced at the pistol inside the plastic bag before the captain tucked it into a cupboard to his right.

"If I need to," the captain said, "I can say you forced me to do this, with my own gun."

"An illegal gun," Daniel said.

"Given the scale of things," the captain said with a look at Daniel, "I hardly think that will matter."

"You're probably right."

A sudden pang of fear threatened to spoil everything, but he wouldn't let it. He looked at Nivi, her head trembling, and felt a charge of excitement once again. It threatened to consume him, and he searched again for that fear in his gut, that things might not go to plan, and he found the balance, the focus he needed to execute his plan with a clear mind. And then, he realised, it was time, as the crewman opened the door of the wheelhouse, and lowered fenders on a long rope between his boat and the trawler.

The fresh air roused Nivi, and the captain idled the boat, clicking the gears into neutral.

"Make it quick," he said, as he scanned the docks for signs of activity. He saw only ravens and a single light in the office of the harbour master, partly obscured as it was by a stack of shipping containers.

Daniel gripped Nivi's arm, dragged her onto her feet and pushed her down the ladder. The crewman had a long gaff, hooked around the railings of Daniel's boat, and a ladder hanging over the side of the trawler. Nivi's shoes skittered on the icy deck, and she would have slipped if the crewman had not reached out and caught her with his spare hand. He let go just as quickly, as if she was a disease and he was now infected. Daniel slid his shoes across the deck and forced Nivi down the ladder. He felt the muscles in his arm tremble as he clutched the rope between her wrists and lowered her onto the deck of his boat. He let go and she crashed onto the deck, too dazed to run. Daniel slid down the ladder, grabbed Nivi by the hair, and pulled her to the covered cockpit. He fumbled with the lock of the cabin door, and then thrust Nivi inside as soon as it was open.

"Hey," the crewman called out. "You're forgetting something."

"Just wait," Daniel said. He ducked inside the cabin, and kneeled on Nivi as he pulled a small holdall out of a storage space and carried it onto the deck. The crewman used the hook of the gaff to take the holdall from Daniel's hands and lift it onboard the trawler. Daniel tapped his leg as the crewman unzipped the holdall, nodded at Daniel and gave a thumbs-up to the captain. Daniel had barely acknowledged the crewman before the captain clicked the trawlers engines into reverse and backed away from the dock.

Daniel reached inside the cabin and grabbed an insulated floatation suit and a pair of thick rubber boots. He pulled on his sailing gear, tossed his city shoes inside the cabin, and locked the door. Daniel sat in the captain's chair, primed and started the engine, and let it idle as he untied the ropes and slipped his boat free of the quay. He grinned as his boat bobbed in the wake of the trawler.

The icefjord in Ilulissat might have made the town famous, especially in the fervour of interest in global warming, but Daniel was about to put the town on a very different map, as the starting point of a most wicked and deeply satisfying act of cruelty. His only regret, he realised, was not knowing what he would do after he was finished with Nivi Winther.

The twinge of excitement he felt, combined with the flush of adrenaline in his body, reassured him that he didn't really care.

Daniel clicked the motorboat into gear and pointed the nose out of the harbour towards the open sea. The pink glow of the sun was fusing with the blue sky above the gargantuan bergs of the fjord, but Daniel was far too focussed on the thoughts of what he had hidden in the cabin of his boat to worry about the start of a beautiful Arctic day in Greenland. The long winter dark might be another month or two away, but for some people, the darkness had already descended, and the world had turned black as death.

Chapter 20

Maratse had to admit that the Commissioner made an impressive entrance when he strode into the emergency room at Dronning Ingrid's Infirmary, flanked as he was by Gaba and Miki in full SRU kit. After a cursory glance at Maratse and Petra, Lars Andersen asked the hospital staff to leave the room and pointed at Gaba.

"Status on Malik Uutaaq?" he said.

"Confused and confessing," Gaba said, "but unhurt."

"Confessing to what?"

"Sleeping with the First Minister's daughter."

"Any comment on the clothing, the jacket found on Tinka Winther?"

"None. He doesn't know how it got there."

"All right," the Commissioner said, drumming his fingers on his thigh. He glanced at the door, and gestured for Miki to stand next to it. "Second," he said, and pointed at Petra. "Status?"

"On the First Minister?" she asked.

"On you, Sergeant, and," he said, with a nod at Maratse, "on our special Constable, here."

"We're fine."

"Good to go?"

"Yes," Petra said. She looked at Maratse, and he nodded.

The Commissioner gestured for Gaba to step closer, and lowered his voice. "Here's what's happened since Petra and Maratse arrived in the ambulance. Gaba, fill me in if I forget anything."

"Yes, sir."

The Commissioner took a breath, and began.

"Since the debate and the apprehending of Malik Uutaaq, we believe that Daniel Tukku has abducted the First Minister. His motive, at this time is unknown, as are his whereabouts, or those of Nivi Winther. However, we believe them to be together. We strongly suspect that they are at sea, most likely in a fishing trawler. How am I doing, Gaba?"

"Just fine, sir," Gaba said. He adjusted the Heckler & Koch MP5 slung around his chest. "I can add that a black Dodge RAM, belonging to Malik Uutaaq, was found on the quay down at the docks. Malik's wife, Naala Uutaaq, confirmed that it was stolen from the parking area at the Katuaq Cultural Centre, sometime during the debate. The panel on the driver's side shows signs of an impact that fits with the description of the collision Petra and Maratse were involved in. The occupants of the car have yet to be identified, but I think we can all agree that there is a high chance it was Tukku and the First Minister."

Maratse longed for a cigarette, but put the thought from his mind, as he thought about what they knew was true, what they supposed was going to happen. It all depended, he realised, on where Tukku was taking the First Minister. An idea began to grow in Maratse's mind, and it made sense if, as he believed, Daniel Tukku had shifted his focus from political power to something more perverse. Petra shot him a quizzical look, but he kept the thought to himself.

"Until we can confirm their location, we have two choices," the Commissioner said, "and I don't like either of them."

"Go on, sir," said Gaba.

"One," he said. "We wait. We put as many eyes

on the docks and airports as possible, but I don't have to tell any of you, that it will take time and it will stretch our resources. If Nivi Winther is still in Nuuk, we can do a house-to-house search, and I am ready to do that, but as soon as word gets out that we are searching for her, we risk forcing Daniel to do something stupid. It could get ugly. Waiting, in the hope that this is a hostage situation, may be the smartest thing to do. It just doesn't feel particularly proactive."

"What's the second option, sir?" Petra asked.

"We get a small team aboard the King Air, ready to fly and intercept Daniel, and bring the First Minister home safely."

"My team is ready, sir."

"I know, Gaba," the Commissioner said. "We just don't know where to send them. Unless anyone has any ideas?"

"I think Maratse does," Petra said. "He has been the least distracted by the drama surrounding Malik Uutaaq. I think he might be able to point us in the right direction."

Maratse looked at Petra for a moment, as she mouthed the word *sorry*, and then he turned to the Commissioner. "Inussuk," he said. "He's taking her back to the scene of the crime."

"What crime?"

"The murder of Tinka Winther," Maratse said.

The Commissioner drummed his fingers again as he processed Maratse's hunch. He looked at Gaba. "What do you think?"

"If they sailed through the night?" he said, and shrugged. "Rain won't stop them, and the weather up north is good at the moment. They could get as far as

Ilulissat, still further tomorrow, if we let them."

"If we let them?" the Commissioner said. "Explain."

"Stopping a trawler at night, at sea, will be dangerous. Better to get them on land, or in a more controlled environment."

"Such as?"

"If Maratse is right," Gaba said, "then it just might be that he intends to do something drastic in a place that is important to him. If he did kill the girl then it is likely that Inussuk and Uummannaq fjord is exactly where he will be headed. With good weather, good seas, and enough fuel, he can easily get there by the end of tomorrow."

"So," the Commissioner said, "you're saying that Tukku can be in Inussuk by Monday evening."

"Late afternoon at the earliest," Gaba said.

The Commissioner walked to the bed Petra was sitting on, and gestured for her to give him some room. He sat down as she moved and looked at Maratse.

"You think he will take her to Inussuk?"

"*Iiji*," Maratse said. He thought about it for a second, and then nodded.

"Gaba? Can you control that environment?"

"If we get there in good time, put a few boats in the water…" He shrugged. "Our biggest advantage would be surprise. But, sir, if he is going to do something to the First Minister, he could do it at any time. Worst case? We don't even find her body."

The Commissioner looked at Maratse again, gauging what he knew of his past, and wondering at his intuition. Maratse returned the Commissioner's look and rested his hands in his lap. The

Commissioner gave Maratse a thin smile and then glanced at the door.

"Miki," he said, "come over here for a minute."

Miki adjusted his MP5 and walked over to stand beside Gaba. The heavy tread of his boots squeaked on the linoleum floor.

"Sir," he said, and waited for the Commissioner to speak.

"Here's the plan," the Commissioner said. "Gaba, split your team in two. I'll keep one half in Nuuk, ready to assist in the house-to-house." Gaba nodded, as the Commissioner continued. "The four of you will fly to Qaarsut." The Commissioner lifted his hand as Gaba started to protest. "I am reinstating Constable Maratse for this one particular operation." He looked at Maratse, and said, "I'll get the paperwork drawn up as soon as we're done here, if, that is, you're willing to go with the team?"

Maratse nodded.

"Good," the Commissioner said. He unbuckled his utility belt and gave it to Maratse. "You can take my gun."

"Sir," Gaba said.

"You've got operational command, Gaba. Don't worry about that. But coordinate with the Uummannaq police, and see if they have a boat available. Have them meet you at the airport in Qaarsut. I'll have the hospital send two medics on the flight, so you have a team of six. Can you work with that?"

"Yes, sir," Gaba said. He turned to Miki and told him to bring the car to the door. When he was gone, Gaba looked at the Commissioner. "I think it is a mistake to bring Maratse in on this."

"It's my decision, Gaba."

"Yes, sir, but," he said with a glance at Maratse, "he is still recovering from whatever it is that happened to him. I need to know I can rely on every member of my team."

"Come on, Gaba," Petra said.

"It's okay," Maratse said. He gritted his teeth and slid off the side of the bed. Maratse picked up the Commissioner's utility belt, and buckled it around his waist. "Gaba is right. I am still recovering, but," he said, and flashed a toothy grin as he patted the belt at his waist, "now I am whole again."

"And ready to go?" the Commissioner said.

"*Iiji*," Maratse said. He nodded at the door, and said, "After you, Gaba."

Maratse bit back a gasp at the sudden flare of pain in his legs, and did his best to match the pace of the SRU leader to the police car. Gaba climbed into the passenger seat, as Petra and Maratse got into the back. Miki shifted the Toyota into first gear and waved at the ambulance to follow. He turned on the emergency lights and the siren and accelerated away from the hospital, cutting through traffic all the way to the airport.

Gaba gave radio commands to the remainder of his team in Nuuk, pausing once or twice to make a note of one detail or another.

Maratse pointed at the number of blue lights flashing at the entrance to the housing areas of Nuuk as the police began their search from one house to the next. The police department, Maratse realised, would be stretched to the limit. The blue lights faded from view as Miki turned onto the road leading to the airport, and accelerated out of the curve in the road at the end of the runway. Petra pointed at the Beechcraft King Air outside the hangar, navigation lights flashing. The gates were open, and Miki drove straight up to the aircraft, with the ambulance a second behind him. The team grabbed their gear from the vehicles, and boarded the plane. Four minutes later and they were in the air and flying north to Qaarsut, the gravel landing strip on the Uummannaq peninsula, just south of the settlement of Inussuk.

Maratse sat next to Petra and dozed as they flew north, waking briefly as Gaba confirmed that a trawler from Nuuk had been seen in Ilulissat a short time ago. Maratse looked out of the window, and realised he had slept for longer than he thought, as the sky brightened with a polar glow of pink and blue. They landed shortly after. Simonsen met them at the airport and drove them down to the hotel boat moored at the jetty, at one end of the beach in Qaarsut.

"You're back," Simonsen said to Maratse, as he gave him a hand onto the boat. "And with a gun?"

"Reinstated," Maratse said. "Temporarily."

"Is there a problem?" Gaba asked.

Simonsen paused for a moment, and then shook his head. He found a seat at the rear of the boat beside the driver.

As soon as everyone was onboard, Miki released the ropes and they pulled away from the jetty. Gaba waited until they were seated, before he started his briefing.

"We're expecting a boat from Ilulissat – large enough to manage a journey like that, so you don't have to worry about spotting anything that looks like a dinghy. It's probably white. As far as we know there are two people onboard, and yes, one of them is likely to be the First Minister."

"So, it's true then?" Simonsen said. "She has been abducted."

"That's what we think, yes." Gaba steadied himself with a hand on a seat as the driver increased power to move away from the wash of an iceberg rolling close to shore. "However, if we get a confirmed sighting somewhere else, then the objective is to get back to the airport as fast as possible." He paused to look at each member of the team, staring at Maratse for a moment, before looking away.

"What if we do see the boat?" asked one of the paramedics.

"We close the distance, as fast as possible," Gaba said, and glanced at the driver of the boat. The man nodded, and Gaba continued. "We'll hail the boat, and we will board it as efficiently as possible. That's Miki and me, if anyone is in doubt. Sergeant Jensen has command on this boat."

Petra identified herself with a wave of her hand. She slapped Maratse lightly on the thigh. "I'm in charge," she whispered.

"On the boat," he said.

"Sure, as soon as he is gone."

"You're going to push him overboard?"

"I might," she said, and grinned.

"When you're done, Sergeant," Gaba said. He looked at Miki, asked if he had forgotten anything, and then looked at his watch. "With the weather conditions as good as they are, we can expect them anytime from early afternoon. So, have some coffee, have a snack, but stay alert." He walked down the centre of the boat between the seats, and stopped beside the driver, describing what he thought would be a good course to sail, sweeping the mouth of the fjord to Inussuk and back again.

Petra stood up to get a coffee. Maratse worked his way to the bow of the boat, and stepped outside onto the small deck. He stood to one side and stuffed his hands inside the pockets of his jacket. The weight of the USP Compact pistol on his hip was familiar, as was the taste of the cigarette he rolled into the gap between his teeth. Petra opened the door and joined him on the deck, pressing a coffee into his hand. They scanned the water as they sipped coffee. Maratse finished his cigarette and flicked the butt into the sea.

"I can see why you like it here," Petra said. "It's beautiful. Peaceful."

"You could visit, when this is over," Maratse said.

"I'd like that."

An iceberg bigger than a shopping mall blocked their view of the mouth of the fjord. Gaba directed the driver around it. The cold air peeled off the iceberg in thick, heavy layers, and the spotters on the deck and the roof shivered in the breath of ice. Petra's hair turned white at the tips, and Maratse felt the familiar tickle in his nose, as the temperature dropped.

From the first dusting of snow at Tinka Winther's funeral, winter had crept down the mountain, from the white peaks of the summit, to the granite walls just above the settlement. The descent of winter could be measured in metres and degrees, but for all its beauty and brightness the winter would be dark, bleak, and cold. Some might call it unforgiving.

Petra was the first to spot the motorboat as it sailed around the tip of the Uummannaq peninsula, unaware that it was the same moment that Nivi had leaped straight into the dark mouth of winter, and was begging for her life.

Ataasinngorneq

MONDAY

Chapter 21

The dark interior of the cabin was a conjuring pit of demons, an evil womb, pulsing on the outside with the rush of water along the hull. Inside it was fetid, with the premonition of death. Nivi could hear the clump of Daniel's boots on deck as he moved around, and, in between, she thought she heard him talk to himself, and sometimes shout. Gone was her shrewd assistant, the devious operator, a force of reckoning on the Greenlandic political stage. Gone was the thirty-something career-driven man, hungry for power, and in his stead was the deviant. She knew that, but she hadn't been prepared for the change, had not seen it grow and consume him. It was as if the devil drove the demon inside. The worlds had been bridged, lines of communication established, serviced with a constant stream of hellish impulse and desire.

Nivi tugged at the tape glued across her mouth. Her skin around the edge of the tape was sore, swollen, an allergic reaction to the glue. An abstract thought reminded her of a similar allergy Tinka had to the tubes of glue they used in schools. And, if she dug farther back into her own childhood, she could trace the same irritation and skin rash when helping her father patch a hole in his boat.

Fibreglass, that was it. She recalled the feel of the fibres, like strands of hair sprayed with a fixing agent, pliable but strong. She had watched her father prepare the formula in the shade cast by his boat. His face, sun-engraved with weather-beaten lines and wrinkles beneath a saggy cloth cap. His hands, rough, the pads of his fingers scored by rope, knife, and hook. The smell of his hands tickled Nivi's nose, as she remembered dark blood in the creases, seal blood, rich and liver-like, fishy. That part of her brain that was detached from her situation was amused that she would find comfort in the memory of her father. What were Tinka's last thoughts, she wondered. Did she think of her father? The man who was supposed to make her feel safe, to protect her?

Nivi shifted her focus to a more immediate concern – breathing. She tugged at a corner of the tape, closed her eyes as she felt her skin around her mouth begin to lift. She tasted blood as the tape tore at her lips, and then it was free, and she gulped the fetid air of the cabin into her lungs. Nivi rolled onto her back, saw the shadow of Daniel's boots through the smoked-glass door, and froze, eyes transfixed to the one part of her captor that she could see, although his demonic face was foremost in her mind.

It appeared then, the face of the demon, as Daniel bent down to peer through the glass door. He stared at Nivi, squinting as he gauged her status, her level of consciousness. And then he saw it, she realised at once, the minute his body stiffened and he stood up. He could see she had removed the tape. Nivi's body reacted with a flood of adrenaline, charging through her veins, pulsing at the tips of her fingers. Her breath changed to short pulses, in and out of her lungs, as Daniel unlocked the door and dropped down into the cabin.

He sat on his haunches, his neck hidden as the thick padding of the suit swelled over his torso. The image of an ape flashed through Nivi's mind, fitting as it was with the primal fear flooding her body. She remembered a wildlife programme on television, primates hunting, branches crashing above the jungle floor, leaves and vines twisting down to the lowest and darkest levels, furthest from the sun. She was on the jungle floor, she realised, where the air was thickest, the odour rankest. She had fallen from the upper levels, she had cascaded. She was prey, to be toyed with, and disposed of. She held her breath, and the hunter spoke.

"You're awake," he said. Daniel removed the fleece hat from his head and stuffed it into the thigh pocket of his overalls. "That's good, because we are close, and I want you to see everything." He licked a bubble of saliva from the corner of his mouth.

"What do you want me to see, Daniel?"

"Ah," he said and wagged his finger, "wonderful things, things that can only be seen with the certain…" He paused to search for the appropriate word. "Stimulus. That's it."

"Daniel, I need to know," Nivi said, her words measured and slow, as she compensated for the rush of chemicals in her body, urging her to flee. She had projected her worst fears onto Malik Uutaaq, in anticipation of the truth that he killed her daughter. Now, faced with the man she believed murdered Tinka, it was almost anticlimactic. She had to know, even if the truth would strip away her last vestige of defence, and she would succumb to the fear. She still had to know.

"Yes," Daniel said, "it was here. She was right here, laying where you are, actually." He swept his hand in the air between them, as if caressing her body.

Tinka's body, Nivi realised, not mine.

"Whatever power Uutaaq might have had over your daughter, I took away when I had her here. I stole it," he said, and reached into another pocket. He pulled out a pair of topaz panties, stretched them between his fingers, and sniffed the length of them. Nivi watched him, and he caught her eye. "These were hers," he said. "Of course, she had already left the nest, a young woman, independent. I bet you never saw these in the wash basket, never hung them on the line." Daniel leaned forwards, and said, "You never knew your daughter like I did, Nivi."

"You're an animal," Nivi whispered.

"I suppose I am," he said, and bunched Tinka's underwear within his fist. "And animals," he said, as he knelt in front of Nivi, "have needs." The punches came at her again and again, until the blood spluttered from her mouth.

The boat spun slowly in the water, and he looked up through the open door as the mountains of the peninsula came into the view, and the witches' hat peak of Qilertinnguit stood tall and proud above Inussuk.

"Look, Nivi," Daniel said and beckoned for her to look out of the door. He grabbed her by the hair when she didn't move, dragging her onto his knee. He pulled her head up, stuck one hand beneath her jaw and lifted her chin. "Do you see that? Do you see the antenna? You can just see the white picket fence. That's the graveyard where your daughter lies. I have brought you home, to bring you together. It's time for you to be reunited."

Nivi tried to turn her head, gasping for breath, and snorting blood from her nose. The top of her left ear creased within the folds of his overalls, but her right ear was unhindered, and free to hear the sound of a motor, and the screech of feedback through a set of speakers, before a voice cut across the surface of the water.

"Daniel Tukku. This is the police."

"No," Daniel whispered. He thrust Nivi to one side, and lifted his head to peer over the lip of the cabin door. He ducked down again, as the voice on the loudspeaker called out his name once more. "No," he shouted.

Nivi watched as Daniel closed and locked the cabin door from the inside. She curled away from him, looped her arms over her knees, stretching the ropes binding her wrists. Daniel stooped to look out of through the glass again, ducking down as a shadow passed the cabin door. He kneeled on the floor and opened a storage panel. It was shaped in a V and Nivi could see lengths of ballast shaped to fit in the bottom of the compartment, flush with the keel. Daniel removed the ballast, heaved it to one side, lips moving as he muttered, and grabbed an axe with a short metal handle. He raised it and struck at the fibreglass at the bottom of the compartment.

"No, Daniel," Nivi shouted. She moved, as he swung the axe again and again, chipping away at the hull of his boat. He stopped at the sound of her voice, turned and swung the axe, catching her on the side of her head with the flat of the adze, a hammer blow that sent her sprawling against the far wall of the cabin. Daniel struck at the hull again as Nivi lifted her hands to her head. Her breath caught in her throat as she felt and heard the shift and crackle of bone beneath the skin just above her ear. Daniel raised the axe again, and again, until the first spray of icy sea water splashed on the front of his overalls.

"Yes," he shouted. "We are going to be all right,

Nivi." He turned to glance at her, frowning for a second at the blood pulsing from the side of her head, and then he grinned. "I will take to your daughter."

Daniel looked up at the sound of a motor in the water, looping around his boat. He raised the axe and chopped at the hull until the water plumed through two holes. He jammed the edge of the axe into one of the holes and prised at the tear, twisting the axe in all directions until the hole was bigger, and water swelled into the storage compartment and flooded into the cabin. He stood up as the water reached his knees, and stared at the hole, at once pleased and frightened that he had succeeded, and that his boat was sinking.

Daniel heard the police call his name once more, knelt in the water and lifted the axe, splashing with each swing. Nivi felt the water on her face and tried to move towards the cabin door. Daniel reached out to catch her arm and held on, swinging the axe with the other hand. If he heard the impact of boots on the deck above, it didn't register on his face.

"Nivi," he said, the words trembling as the cold water seeped into his overalls, rising over his knees to submerge his thighs. "Do you know what I called your daughter, just before I pushed her over the side of this boat?"

"No," Nivi whispered. She tried to move out of the water. Daniel pinched her arm in his grip. She looked through the glass door, and stared into the barrel of a submachine gun, as the policeman moved to the left and the right, searching for a clear shot. Daniel lifted the axe again, and lost his balance as the axe plunged through the hull. He let go of Nivi, recovered his balance, and pulled the axe out of the water.

"I called her a Greenlandic bitch," he said, and reached for Nivi. "No, wait," he said, and frowned. "I said she should speak Greenlandic, *bitch*. That's what I said." He pulled Nivi close and she saw the blue tinge to his lips as the cold gripped his body. "I was being Malik," he said. "You understand? Don't you?"

"Yes," Nivi said. She looked up at the tramp of boots on the roof of the cabin. A shadow appeared above the skylight window, and then a masked face, and the barrel of another gun.

"It was an act," Daniel said. "Of course it was." The twitch of muscles in Daniel's face settled and his cheeks smoothed as he exhaled. He stroked the side of Nivi's face. "You're hurt?"

"Yes," she said. "Let me go, Daniel."

"Let you go?"

"Yes."

Daniel rested his hand on the butt of the axe handle. He stroked her face again, and said, "You have your daughter's eyes."

"Let me go," Nivi whispered.

Daniel nodded, and said, "Yes. Why not? I could do it."

"Please."

"I could do it for Tinka," he said, and shrugged, "to make amends."

"Daniel," said a voice from the deck of the boat. "You need to come out now."

Daniel shivered. He reached around Nivi and unlocked the cabin door. He stumbled in the water as he grabbed Nivi by the hair at the back of her head, and said, "Up." He pulled her to her feet and pushed her up the steps to the deck, forcing the masked policeman to take a step back, towards the railings.

Daniel held the axe tight in his right hand, shoved Nivi forwards, propelling her into the policeman's chest as he raised the axe and roared.

The policeman let go of the submachine gun attached to his chest, and wrapped his arms around Nivi. The force of Nivi's momentum pushed the policeman over the side of the boat, and he pulled the First Minister with him. The weight of his equipment dragged them below the surface as his partner took aim from the cabin roof, and fired a burst of three bullets into Daniel's back. The axe clattered across the deck as Daniel crashed into the railings, reaching for Nivi as she disappeared within Gaba's grasp into the black sea flecked with ice.

"Gaba," Miki shouted from the cabin roof. He pulled the mask from his face and leaped onto the deck of the boat. He flung his body at the railings, looking up as Maratse tossed his utility belt onto the deck of the hotel boat, threw his jacket to one side, and dived into the water.

Maratse ignored the cold clamp around his chest and grabbed at the clothes on Nivi's back, pulling the First Minister free of Gaba's grip, and propelling her to the surface. He took another stroke downwards as the SRU leader clawed at the equipment on his chest. Maratse grabbed Gaba's vest and kicked. He kicked through the explosion of pain firing through the nerves in his legs, ignored the vice of cold pinching his head, and kicked for the surface. Gaba fumbled with the clasp of his helmet, cut the sling of his weapon with a knife and kicked with Maratse until they breached the surface, grasping each other with stiff fingers as Petra and Miki stretched over the side of the hotel boat, beneath the railings, and hauled them to safety.

Miki peeled the equipment and clothes from his boss, wrapping him in a blanket, as Petra did the same for Maratse. The paramedics triaged their patients, treating them in turn for trauma and exposure. Petra helped Maratse into a chair next to the First Minister. She kissed him on the forehead and made room for Gaba.

Nivi slid her hand out from beneath her blanket to clutch Maratse's fingers. She turned her bandaged head and looked at him. "Thank you, Constable."

"*Iiji,*" Maratse said. "You're welcome."

"I'm not going to hold your hand," Gaba said, and nudged Maratse from the other side, "but thank you."

Maratse bit through the pain in his legs and nodded.

Marlunngorneq

TUESDAY

Chapter 22

Maratse woke to the sound of Petra coming down the stairs. He lifted his head as she walked into the living room, stopping in the doorway to wave.

"Did you sleep?" she asked.

"*Iiji.*"

"Much pain?"

He nodded and lowered his head, as Petra walked into the kitchen. He listened as she boiled water for coffee, and tutted at the lack of food in the fridge, and the empty cupboards.

"I'm going shopping," she said, putting a mug of coffee on the table next to Maratse. "See if you can get dressed."

Maratse nodded, waiting until she had left before he propped himself up on the sofa and reached for the mug. He grimaced at the pain in his legs, and then shrugged. He had to live with it, he reasoned, but it didn't have to define him, or determine what he did and didn't do with his life. Maratse's temporary reinstatement in the police had expired as soon as the Commissioner was briefed on the status of the operation. Maratse contemplated his second retirement in as many weeks, as he sipped his coffee, and listened to the puppy scratching at the deck outside the house. It tumbled up and down the length of the deck as Petra returned with bacon, eggs, and bread.

"He's so cute," Petra said, pausing for a moment to talk to the puppy. She knocked the snow from her boots, kicking them off and walking through to the lounge.

"He's a she."

"And does she have a name yet?"

"*Eeqqi*," Maratse said. "I'm working on it."

Maratse dressed, as Petra made breakfast. He looked out of the window as Karl and Edvard walked down to the dock to meet the hotel boat as it bumped against the jetty. Nivi Winther stepped off the boat, together with Simonsen and Danielsen from Uummannaq.

"Is that them?" Petra called from the kitchen.

"*Iji.*"

"And what time is the press conference?"

"In an hour."

"Okay," Petra said, as she put two plates with bacon sandwiches on the table. She beckoned for Maratse to come and eat, waited until he sat down, and then said, "I'm curious as to why she is holding it here, not in Nuuk."

The same thought had kept Maratse awake for the first part of the night, until the painkillers had kicked in. He had given the dark nature of his dreams a name, called it trauma, and set it to one side. Releasing a statement about her daughter's killer beside her grave, he imagined, must be Nivi Winther's way of working through her trauma. Although, he did wonder if she had other plans, a different agenda. She was a strong woman, all the stronger for bouncing back from the death of her daughter, and her own abduction.

"You're far away again," Petra said, when she was finished with her sandwich. She sipped her coffee and watched Maratse eat.

"This is good."

"I know," she said.

They both looked up at the sound of a plane

passing overhead to land at the gravel strip in Qaarsut. It coincided with the departure of the hotel boat, and Maratse wondered again if Nivi was planning something.

"Gaba called when I was in the store," Petra said. "He wanted me to say hi."

"Hmm," Maratse said. "How is Miki?"

"He's fine. Filling in forms and being interviewed in Nuuk. It's the first time for him, killing a man, but the union has his back, and there were plenty of witnesses."

"Good." Maratse finished his breakfast. He looked out of the window as Karl, Edvard, and the policemen followed Nivi up the path to the graveyard. "I'll need longer today," he said, "to walk up the mountain."

"Sure," Petra said. "Do you want to go now?"

"*Iiji*," Maratse said, and stood up. He walked to the door, pulled on his jacket, and stuffed his feet into his boots.

The puppy lifted its head as Maratse and Petra walked out of the house. Maratse growled at it, and Petra laughed as the puppy danced back to where it was lying at the end of the deck.

"You have a way with dogs, eh?"

"She's a good dog," Maratse said.

"One that needs a name. You can't call it *she* or *it* for the rest of its life."

"Why not?"

"You just can't," Petra said and walked down the steps. She waited for Maratse on the beach, scuffing the snow to one side to reveal the black sand and shells beneath. They walked towards the path, and started to climb the mountainside.

When they reached the top, Maratse stopped to light a cigarette. He nodded at Nivi as she stood beside the grave of her daughter. Petra tugged his elbow and pointed at the hotel boat on its way back from the airport. The boat was stuffed with passengers.

"So," she said, "any ideas?"

"None," Maratse said, and rolled the cigarette into the gap between his teeth. He smoked for a minute more, snubbed the half-finished cigarette between his finger and thumb, and pushed it back into the packet. He spotted a flash of white fur bounding up the path, and growled at the puppy to stay put. He turned his back on it, and walked with Petra to the entrance to the graveyard. When he looked back at the puppy, it was sitting up straight by the side of the path, its head flicking back and forth between the guests arriving for the funeral. Maratse noticed that most of them carried cameras of various sizes, one of which was a digital video camera.

"The press," he said, and nudged Petra. The photographers moved to one side to take photographs of the last people in the group.

"That's Malik Uutaaq, and his family," Petra said. "What is she planning?"

Malik glanced at Petra and Maratse as he walked past them. He held his wife's hand on one side, and his daughter on the other. Sipu, his son, played with the puppy, until his father stopped and called for him.

Qitu Kalia separated himself from the photographers and journalists to shake Maratse's hand, before rejoining the group that Nivi Winther had assembled in the snow beside five open graves. She stood beside her daughter's grave. The loose sheets of her notes flapped in the wind.

"You're all wondering," she said in Greenlandic, her voice crisp and clear like the air, "why I have you invited you here. The simple answer is, I want my daughter to hear what I have to say." Cameras started to click, and she held up her hand for them to wait. The film crew kept rolling, and Maratse realised she must have asked for that. "Daniel Tukku was my colleague, he was my friend, and he was also the man who murdered my daughter." Nivi paused to wipe a tear from her cheek. "She is safe now, but her death and suffering make me think of all the people suffering in Greenland, even people like Daniel Tukku. He was Greenlandic, just like my Tinka was." Nivi waited for the journalists and photographers to finish taking notes and pictures. "When I visit my daughter, to talk to her about the whales in the fjord, and to imagine the life she might have led, I will also tell her about Greenland and the Greenlandic people. As First Minister of Greenland I have a responsibility to care for all Greenlanders, we all do. But, as First Minister, I failed in my duty to give Daniel the help he needed. I will be reminded of that every time I visit Tinka."

Nivi looked over her shoulder, as if to take strength from the power of the ice in the fjord, to draw on winter's strengths, so that she need not dwell on its hardships. She looked back, and caught Maratse's eye, smiling as she continued with her speech.

"Tinka is safe, but how safe do we feel? How safe are we as a nation, as a people, as Greenlanders?" Nivi beckoned for Malik to come and stand beside her. She embraced him as he walked up to her, and took his hand as he turned to face his family, and the press, and the people of Greenland. "I asked Malik Uutaaq to join me here on this difficult day, because when one has experienced the darkest side of human nature, the darkest side of Greenland, it is important to reach out and embrace all that is good about Greenland, and to go forwards into the dark of winter, with a new heart, a new focus, and a new leadership. Which is why, I am pleased to say, Malik Uutaaq and I have agreed to work together to bring our people together, and to embrace a new Greenland for all Greenlanders." Nivi paused at a renewed frenzy of cameras clicking. "So when you vote in May next year, we can promise you an exciting election, and furthermore, we can promise a stable, political vision, built on trust and common ground embracing the true Greenlandic identity for all Greenlanders."

Maratse felt Petra take his hand, as Nivi repeated her speech in Danish. "Piitalaat," he said, as he felt her tremble. "Are you all right?"

"Yes," she whispered. "I am now."

The press stayed as Nivi rearranged the flowers on her daughter's grave. Maratse didn't know if the camera caught the look in her eye, but he saw a spark of hope between the tears.

Petra held Maratse's hand long after the last journalist had followed Nivi and Malik down the mountain path and back to the hotel boat. He imagined that there would be a question and answer session at the hotel in Uummannaq, and was pleased that the press, politicians and policemen were leaving. He tugged at Petra's hand and they walked over to Tinka Winther's grave. Karl and Edvard joined them.

"Five graves left," Karl said, as he lit a cigarette.

Maratse lit his own and Petra stepped to one side to admire the view and avoid the smoke. She walked back to Maratse as Karl and Edvard finished their cigarettes and walked down the path to Inussuk.

"So," she said, "what are you going to do now?"

"Retire," he said, and shrugged.

"You've tried that already."

"*Iiji.*"

"Perhaps you should try a new approach?"

Petra smiled as the puppy bounded into the graveyard and sat at the foot of Tinka's grave.

"You said it was a she?" Petra said.

"It is."

"And she needs a name." Petra nodded at the puppy. "Tinka. How about that?"

Maratse looked at the puppy as it flicked its head between him and Petra. He took a breath and gritted his teeth as he bent down onto his knees. The puppy looked at him, watched him, and then bounded across the snow into his lap when Maratse clicked his tongue.

"A few more, and you've got a team," Petra said.

"Karl's son has more dogs he wants to get rid of," Maratse said, "and a boat he wants to sell."

Petra looked out at the fjord, took a deep breath, and nodded. "So, you've decided then, you're going to be a hunter."

"Hunting and fishing," Maratse said. He curled the puppy's ears between his fingers and thumbs. "Or maybe just sledging."

"I'd like to try that," Petra said.

"Come back in spring. My team will be ready."

"You won't come back to Nuuk?"

Maratse let go of the puppy and looked at Petra.

He could feel the puppy's claws on his thighs, and the needle-like points of its milk teeth as it nibbled at his fingers.

"I don't think so."

"You're sure?"

"*Iiji*," he said. "This is where I belong."

AUTHOR'S NOTE

Greenland is the largest island in the world, but with roughly 56,000 inhabitants, its population is smaller than the city of Galveston, Texas. The capital of Nuuk has a population of roughly 15,000 people. Some settlements have fewer than one hundred residents. There are no roads connecting the towns, villages, and settlements. Transport to and from the inhabited areas is predominantly serviced by planes with short take-off and landing capabilities, helicopters, and boats. In the areas where the sea ice is thick enough, Greenlanders can travel across the ice in cars, and by snow scooters and dog sledges.

Constable David Maratse's fictive Greenland is affected by the same limitations of the real Greenland. His fictive stories are inspired by some events and many places that exist in Greenland. Most place names are the same, such as Nuuk, and Uummannaq, but used fictitiously. The settlement of Inussuk does not exist, although observant readers looking at a map will be able to take a good guess at where it might be found.

Chris
February 2018
Denmark

ACKNOWLEDGEMENTS

I would like to thank Isabel Dennis-Muir for her invaluable editing skills and feedback on the manuscript. While several people have contributed to *Seven Graves, One Winter*, the mistakes and inaccuracies are all my own.

Chris
February 2018
Denmark

ABOUT THE AUTHOR

Christoffer Petersen is the author's pen name. He lives in Denmark. Chris started writing stories about Greenland while teaching in Qaanaaq, the largest village in the very north of Greenland – the population peaked at 600 during the two years he lived there. Chris spent a total of seven years in Greenland, teaching in remote communities and at the Police Academy in the capital of Nuuk.

Chris continues to be inspired by the vast icy wilderness of the Arctic and his books have a common setting in the region, with a Scandinavian influence. He has also watched enough Bourne movies to no longer be surprised by the plot, but not enough to get bored.

You can find Chris in Denmark or online here:

www.christoffer-petersen.com

SEVEN GRAVES, ONE WINTER

9 788793 680005